Why, what is pomp,
rule, reign, but earth
and dust?
And, live we how we
can, yet die we must

1 3 5 7 9 10 8 6 4 2

Vintage
20 Vauxhall Bridge Road,
London SW1V 2SA

Vintage Classics is part of the Penguin Random House
group of companies whose addresses can be found at
global.penguinrandomhouse.com

 Penguin
Random House
UK

This edition published by Vintage in 2020

penguin.co.uk/vintage

A CIP catalogue record for this book is available from the British Library

ISBN 9781784876098

Typeset in 9.5/14 pt FreightText Pro
by Jouve (UK), Milton Keynes
Printed and bound in Great Britain by Clays Ltd, Elcograf S.p.A.

Penguin Random House is committed to a sustainable future for our
business, our readers and our planet. This book is made from Forest
Stewardship Council® certified paper.

Power

WILLIAM SHAKESPEARE

VINTAGE MINIS

Contents

1. Dreams of Power

'Glamis, and thane of Cawdor!
The greatest is behind.'

From MACBETH

Macbeth and Banquo are returning from a bloody battle where they fought bravely against rebels on behalf of their king, Duncan. On their journey home they encounter three witches.

ACT I, SCENE III

Enter MACBETH *and* BANQUO

MACBETH	So foul and fair a day I have not seen.
BANQUO	How far is't call'd to Forres? What are these
	So wither'd and so wild in their attire,
	That look not like the inhabitants o' the earth,
	And yet are on't? Live you? or are you aught
	That man may question? You seem to understand me,
	By each at once her chappy finger laying
	Upon her skinny lips: you should be women,
	And yet your beards forbid me to interpret
	That you are so.
MACBETH	Speak, if you can: what are you?
FIRST WITCH	All hail, Macbeth! hail to thee, thane of Glamis!
SECOND WITCH	All hail, Macbeth, hail to thee, thane of Cawdor!
THIRD WITCH	All hail, Macbeth, thou shalt be king hereafter!
BANQUO	Good sir, why do you start; and seem to fear
	Things that do sound so fair? I' the name of truth,
	Are ye fantastical, or that indeed
	Which outwardly ye show? My noble partner
	You greet with present grace and great prediction

Of noble having and of royal hope,
That he seems rapt withal: to me you
speak not.
If you can look into the seeds of time,
And say which grain will grow and which
will not,
Speak then to me, who neither beg nor fear
Your favours nor your hate.

FIRST WITCH   Hail!

SECOND WITCH   Hail!

THIRD WITCH   Hail!

FIRST WITCH   Lesser than Macbeth, and greater.

SECOND WITCH   Not so happy, yet much happier.

THIRD WITCH   Thou shalt get kings, though thou be none:
So all hail, Macbeth and Banquo!

FIRST WITCH   Banquo and Macbeth, all hail!

MACBETH   Stay, you imperfect speakers, tell me more:
By Sinel's death I know I am thane of
Glamis;
But how of Cawdor? the thane of Cawdor
lives,
A prosperous gentleman; and to be king
Stands not within the prospect of belief,
No more than to be Cawdor. Say from
whence
You owe this strange intelligence? or why
Upon this blasted heath you stop our way
With such prophetic greeting? Speak, I
charge you.

Witches vanish

BANQUO   The earth hath bubbles, as the water has,
            And these are of them. Whither are they vanish'd?

MACBETH   Into the air; and what seem'd corporal melted
            As breath into the wind. Would they had stay'd!

BANQUO   Were such things here as we do speak about?
            Or have we eaten on the insane root
            That takes the reason prisoner?

MACBETH   Your children shall be kings.

BANQUO   You shall be king.

MACBETH   And thane of Cawdor too: went it not so?

BANQUO   To the selfsame tune and words. Who's here?

Enter ROSS *and* ANGUS

ROSS   The king hath happily received, Macbeth,
            The news of thy success; and when he reads
            Thy personal venture in the rebels' fight,
            His wonders and his praises do contend
            Which should be thine or his: silenced with that,
            In viewing o'er the rest o' the selfsame day,
            He finds thee in the stout Norweyan ranks,
            Nothing afeard of what thyself didst make,
            Strange images of death. As thick as hail
            Came post with post; and every one did bear
            Thy praises in his kingdom's great defence,
            And pour'd them down before him.

ANGUS   We are sent
            To give thee from our royal master thanks;

Only to herald thee into his sight,
Not pay thee.

ROSS   And, for an earnest of a greater honour,
He bade me, from him, call thee thane of Cawdor:
In which addition, hail, most worthy thane!
For it is thine.

BANQUO   What, can the devil speak true?

MACBETH   The thane of Cawdor lives: why do you dress me
In borrow'd robes?

ANGUS   Who was the thane lives yet;
But under heavy judgment bears that life
Which he deserves to lose. Whether he was combined
With those of Norway, or did line the rebel
With hidden help and vantage, or that with both
He labour'd in his country's wreck, I know not;
But treasons capital, confess'd and proved,
Have overthrown him.

MACBETH   [*Aside*]

Glamis, and thane of Cawdor!
The greatest is behind.

To ROSS *and* ANGUS

Thanks for your pains.

To BANQUO

Do you not hope your children shall be kings,
When those that gave the thane of Cawdor to me
Promised no less to them?

BANQUO	That trusted home
	Might yet enkindle you unto the crown,
	Besides the thane of Cawdor. But 'tis strange:
	And oftentimes, to win us to our harm,
	The instruments of darkness tell us truths,
	Win us with honest trifles, to betray's
	In deepest consequence.
	Cousins, a word, I pray you.
MACBETH	[*Aside*]
	Two truths are told,
	As happy prologues to the swelling act
	Of the imperial theme.—I thank you, gentlemen.
	[*Aside*]
	This supernatural soliciting
	Cannot be ill, cannot be good: if ill,
	Why hath it given me earnest of success,
	Commencing in a truth? I am thane of Cawdor:
	If good, why do I yield to that suggestion
	Whose horrid image doth unfix my hair
	And make my seated heart knock at my ribs,
	Against the use of nature? Present fears
	Are less than horrible imaginings:
	My thought, whose murder yet is but fantastical,
	Shakes so my single state of man that function
	Is smother'd in surmise, and nothing is
	But what is not.
BANQUO	Look, how our partner's rapt.
MACBETH	[*Aside*]

	If chance will have me king, why, chance may crown me,
	Without my stir.
BANQUO	New honours come upon him,
	Like our strange garments, cleave not to their mould
	But with the aid of use.
MACBETH	[*Aside*]
	Come what come may,
	Time and the hour runs through the roughest day.
BANQUO	Worthy Macbeth, we stay upon your leisure.
MACBETH	Give me your favour: my dull brain was wrought
	With things forgotten. Kind gentlemen, your pains
	Are register'd where every day I turn
	The leaf to read them. Let us toward the king.
	Think upon what hath chanced, and, at more time,
	The interim having weigh'd it, let us speak
	Our free hearts each to other.
BANQUO	Very gladly.
MACBETH	Till then, enough. Come, friends.

Exeunt

2. Dangerous Ambition

'The fault, dear Brutus, is not in our stars,
But in ourselves, that we are underlings.'

From JULIUS CAESAR

Julius Caesar, the popular ruler of Rome, has emerged victorious from a civil war. A group of senators, including Cassius and Brutus, fear Caesar will make himself king, or ruler for life, changing Rome from a republic into a despotic monarchy.

ACT I, SCENE II

BRUTUS What means this shouting? I do fear, the people
        Choose Caesar for their king.

CASSIUS Ay, do you fear it?
        Then must I think you would not have it so.

BRUTUS I would not, Cassius; yet I love him well.
        But wherefore do you hold me here so long?
        What is it that you would impart to me?
        If it be aught toward the general good,
        Set honour in one eye and death i' the other,
        And I will look on both indifferently,
        For let the gods so speed me as I love
        The name of honour more than I fear death.

CASSIUS I know that virtue to be in you, Brutus,
        As well as I do know your outward favour.
        Well, honour is the subject of my story.
        I cannot tell what you and other men
        Think of this life; but, for my single self,
        I had as lief not be as live to be
        In awe of such a thing as I myself.
        I was born free as Caesar; so were you:
        We both have fed as well, and we can both
        Endure the winter's cold as well as he:
        For once, upon a raw and gusty day,
        The troubled Tiber chafing with her shores,
        Caesar said to me 'Darest thou, Cassius, now
        Leap in with me into this angry flood,

And swim to yonder point?' Upon the word,
Accoutred as I was, I plunged in
And bade him follow; so indeed he did.
The torrent roar'd, and we did buffet it
With lusty sinews, throwing it aside
And stemming it with hearts of controversy;
But ere we could arrive the point proposed,
Caesar cried 'Help me, Cassius, or I sink!'
I, as Aeneas, our great ancestor,
Did from the flames of Troy upon his shoulder
The old Anchises bear, so from the waves of Tiber
Did I the tired Caesar. And this man
Is now become a god, and Cassius is
A wretched creature and must bend his body,
If Caesar carelessly but nod on him.
He had a fever when he was in Spain,
And when the fit was on him, I did mark
How he did shake: 'tis true, this god did shake;
His coward lips did from their colour fly,
And that same eye whose bend doth awe
the world
Did lose his lustre: I did hear him groan:
Ay, and that tongue of his that bade the Romans
Mark him and write his speeches in their books,
Alas, it cried 'Give me some drink, Titinius,'
As a sick girl. Ye gods, it doth amaze me
A man of such a feeble temper should
So get the start of the majestic world
And bear the palm alone.

Shout. Flourish

BRUTUS   Another general shout!
          I do believe that these applauses are
          For some new honours that are heap'd on Caesar.

CASSIUS   Why, man, he doth bestride the narrow world
          Like a Colossus, and we petty men
          Walk under his huge legs and peep about
          To find ourselves dishonourable graves.
          Men at some time are masters of their fates:
          The fault, dear Brutus, is not in our stars,
          But in ourselves, that we are underlings.
          Brutus and Caesar: what should be in that 'Caesar'?
          Why should that name be sounded more than yours?
          Write them together, yours is as fair a name;
          Sound them, it doth become the mouth as well;
          Weigh them, it is as heavy; conjure with 'em,
          Brutus will start a spirit as soon as Caesar.
          Now, in the names of all the gods at once,
          Upon what meat doth this our Caesar feed,
          That he is grown so great? Age, thou art shamed!
          Rome, thou hast lost the breed of noble bloods!
          When went there by an age, since the great flood,
          But it was famed with more than with one man?
          When could they say till now, that talk'd of Rome,
          That her wide walls encompass'd but one man?
          Now is it Rome indeed and room enough,
          When there is in it but one only man.
          O, you and I have heard our fathers say,

There was a Brutus once that would have brook'd
The eternal devil to keep his state in Rome
As easily as a king.

BRUTUS   That you do love me, I am nothing jealous;
What you would work me to, I have some aim:
How I have thought of this and of these times,
I shall recount hereafter; for this present,
I would not, so with love I might entreat you,
Be any further moved. What you have said
I will consider; what you have to say
I will with patience hear, and find a time
Both meet to hear and answer such high things.
Till then, my noble friend, chew upon this:
Brutus had rather be a villager
Than to repute himself a son of Rome
Under these hard conditions as this time
Is like to lay upon us.

3. Succession

'How I came by the crown, O God forgive;
And grant it may with thee in true peace live!'

From HENRY IV, PART II

King Henry IV's reign has been beset by rebellion and war. Meanwhile his son Henry, heir to the throne, haunts the seedier parts of London with undesirable companions. When Prince Henry at last visits his dying father he finds him asleep. Believing him dead, Hal leaves the room with the king's crown. Upon waking, King Henry misunderstands the action, and laments that the prince cannot wait for his father to die.

ACT IV, SCENE V

PRINCE HENRY   I never thought to hear you speak again.

KING HENRY IV   Thy wish was father, Harry, to that thought:
I stay too long by thee, I weary thee.
Dost thou so hunger for mine empty chair
That thou wilt needs invest thee with my
honours
Before thy hour be ripe? O foolish youth!
Thou seek'st the greatness that will
o'erwhelm thee.
Stay but a little; for my cloud of dignity
Is held from falling with so weak a wind
That it will quickly drop: my day is dim.
Thou hast stolen that which after some
few hours
Were thine without offence; and at my death
Thou hast seal'd up my expectation:
Thy life did manifest thou lovedst me not,
And thou wilt have me die assured of it.
Thou hidest a thousand daggers in thy
thoughts,
Which thou hast whetted on thy stony heart,
To stab at half an hour of my life.
What! canst thou not forbear me half an hour?
Then get thee gone and dig my grave thyself,
And bid the merry bells ring to thine ear
That thou art crowned, not that I am dead.

Let all the tears that should bedew
my hearse
Be drops of balm to sanctify thy head:
Only compound me with forgotten dust,
Give that which gave thee life unto the worms.
Pluck down my officers, break my decrees;
For now a time is come to mock at form:
Harry the Fifth is crown'd: up, vanity!
Down, royal state! all you sage counsellors,
hence!
And to the English court assemble now,
From every region, apes of idleness!
Now, neighbour confines, purge you of
your scum:
Have you a ruffian that will swear, drink,
dance,
Revel the night, rob, murder, and commit
The oldest sins the newest kind of ways?
Be happy, he will trouble you no more;
England shall double gild his treble guilt,
England shall give him office, honour, might;
For the fifth Harry from curb'd licence
plucks
The muzzle of restraint, and the wild dog
Shall flesh his tooth on every innocent.
O my poor kingdom, sick with civil blows!
When that my care could not withhold
thy riots,
What wilt thou do when riot is thy care?

O, thou wilt be a wilderness again,
Peopled with wolves, thy old inhabitants!

PRINCE HENRY   O, pardon me, my liege! but for my tears,
The moist impediments unto my speech,
I had forestall'd this dear and deep rebuke
Ere you with grief had spoke and I had heard
The course of it so far. There is your crown;
And He that wears the crown immortally
Long guard it yours! If I affect it more
Than as your honour and as your renown,
Let me no more from this obedience rise,
Which my most inward true and
duteous spirit
Teacheth, this prostrate and exterior
bending.
God witness with me, when I here came in,
And found no course of breath within your
majesty,
How cold it struck my heart! If I do feign,
O, let me in my present wildness die
And never live to show the incredulous
world
The noble change that I have purposed!
Coming to look on you, thinking you dead,
And dead almost, my liege, to think you
were,
I spake unto this crown as having sense,
And thus upbraided it: 'The care on thee
depending

Hath fed upon the body of my father;
Therefore, thou best of gold art worst
of gold:
Other, less fine in carat, is more precious,
Preserving life in medicine potable;
But thou, most fine, most honour'd, most
renown'd,
Hast eat thy bearer up.' Thus, my most
royal liege,
Accusing it, I put it on my head,
To try with it, as with an enemy
That had before my face murder'd
my father,
The quarrel of a true inheritor.
But if it did infect my blood with joy,
Or swell my thoughts to any strain of pride;
If any rebel or vain spirit of mine
Did with the least affection of a welcome
Give entertainment to the might of it,
Let God for ever keep it from my head
And make me as the poorest vassal is
That doth with awe and terror kneel to it!

KING HENRY IV O my son,
God put it in thy mind to take it hence,
That thou mightst win the more thy
father's love,
Pleading so wisely in excuse of it!
Come hither, Harry, sit thou by my bed;
And hear, I think, the very latest counsel

That ever I shall breathe. God knows, my son,
By what by-paths and indirect crook'd ways
I met this crown; and I myself know well
How troublesome it sat upon my head.
To thee it shall descend with bitter quiet,
Better opinion, better confirmation;
For all the soil of the achievement goes
With me into the earth. It seem'd in me
But as an honour snatch'd with
boisterous hand,
And I had many living to upbraid
My gain of it by their assistances;
Which daily grew to quarrel and to
bloodshed,
Wounding supposed peace: all these
bold fears
Thou see'st with peril I have answered;
For all my reign hath been but as a scene
Acting that argument: and now my death
Changes the mode; for what in me was
purchased,
Falls upon thee in a more fairer sort.
So thou the garland wear'st successively.
Yet, though thou stand'st more sure than I
could do,
Thou art not firm enough, since griefs
are green;
And all my friends, which thou must make
thy friends,

Have but their stings and teeth newly
ta'en out;
By whose fell working I was first advanced
And by whose power I well might lodge a fear
To be again displaced: which to avoid,
I cut them off; and had a purpose now
To lead out many to the Holy Land,
Lest rest and lying still might make
them look
Too near unto my state. Therefore, my Harry,
Be it thy course to busy giddy minds
With foreign quarrels; that action, hence
borne out,
May waste the memory of the former days.
More would I, but my lungs are wasted so
That strength of speech is utterly denied me.
How I came by the crown, O God forgive;
And grant it may with thee in true peace live!

PRINCE HENRY My gracious liege,
You won it, wore it, kept it, gave it me;
Then plain and right must my possession be:
Which I with more than with a common pain
'Gainst all the world will rightfully
maintain.

4. Power Enfeebled

'Ah! thus King Henry throws away his crutch
Before his legs be firm to bear his body.'

From HENRY VI, PART II

Henry VI was only nine months old when his popular father died, so the resolutely honourable Duke of Gloucester rules England in his stead as Lord Protector. By the time Henry comes of age, Gloucester has powerful enemies, including the scheming Queen Margaret and her lover the Duke of Suffolk. Not knowing who to trust, the young King is powerless to prevent the downfall of his most loyal servant.

ACT III, SCENE I

Enter KING HENRY VI, QUEEN MARGARET,
CARDINAL, SUFFOLK, YORK, BUCKINGHAM,
SALISBURY *and* WARWICK.

KING HENRY VI   I muse my Lord of Gloucester is not come:
'Tis not his wont to be the hindmost man,
Whate'er occasion keeps him from us now.

QUEEN MARGARET   Can you not see? or will ye not observe
The strangeness of his alter'd
countenance?
With what a majesty he bears himself,
How insolent of late he is become,
How proud, how peremptory, and unlike
himself?
We know the time since he was mild and
affable,
And if we did but glance a far-off look,
Immediately he was upon his knee,
That all the court admired him for
submission:
But meet him now, and, be it in the morn,
When every one will give the time of day,
He knits his brow and shows an
angry eye,
And passeth by with stiff unbowed knee,
Disdaining duty that to us belongs.

Small curs are not regarded when
they grin;
But great men tremble when the lion roars;
And Humphrey is no little man in England.
First note that he is near you in descent,
And should you fall, he as the next
will mount.
Me seemeth then it is no policy,
Respecting what a rancorous mind
he bears
And his advantage following your decease,
That he should come about your
royal person
Or be admitted to your highness' council.
By flattery hath he won the commons'
hearts,
And when he please to make commotion,
'Tis to be fear'd they all will follow him.
Now 'tis the spring, and weeds are
shallow-rooted;
Suffer them now, and they'll o'ergrow
the garden
And choke the herbs for want of
husbandry.
The reverent care I bear unto my lord
Made me collect these dangers in the duke.
If it be fond, call it a woman's fear;
Which fear if better reasons can supplant,
I will subscribe and say I wrong'd the duke.

My Lord of Suffolk, Buckingham,
and York,
Reprove my allegation, if you can;
Or else conclude my words effectual.

SUFFOLK   Well hath your highness seen into
this duke;
And, had I first been put to speak
my mind,
I think I should have told your
grace's tale.
The duchess, by his subornation,
Upon my life, began her devilish
practices:
Or, if he were not privy to those faults,
Yet, by reputing of his high descent,
As next the king he was successive heir,
And such high vaunts of his nobility,
Did instigate the bedlam brain-sick
duchess
By wicked means to frame our
sovereign's fall.
Smooth runs the water where the
brook is deep;
And in his simple show he harbours
treason.
The fox barks not when he would steal
the lamb.
No, no, my sovereign; Gloucester is a man
Unsounded yet and full of deep deceit.

CARDINAL	Did he not, contrary to form of law,
	Devise strange deaths for small
	offences done?
YORK	And did he not, in his protectorship,
	Levy great sums of money through
	the realm
	For soldiers' pay in France, and never
	sent it?
	By means whereof the towns each day
	revolted.
BUCKINGHAM	Tut, these are petty faults to faults
	unknown.
	Which time will bring to light in smooth
	Duke Humphrey.
KING HENRY VI	My lords, at once: the care you have of us,
	To mow down thorns that would annoy
	our foot,
	Is worthy praise: but, shall I speak my
	conscience,
	Our kinsman Gloucester is as innocent
	From meaning treason to our royal person
	As is the sucking lamb or harmless dove:
	The duke is virtuous, mild and too well
	given
	To dream on evil or to work my downfall.
QUEEN MARGARET	Ah, what's more dangerous than this fond
	affiance!
	Seems he a dove? his feathers are but
	borrowed,

For he's disposed as the hateful raven:
Is he a lamb? his skin is surely lent him,
For he's inclined as is the ravenous wolf.
Who cannot steal a shape that means
deceit?
Take heed, my lord; the welfare of us all
Hangs on the cutting short that
fraudful man.

Enter SOMERSET

SOMERSET	All health unto my gracious sovereign!
KING HENRY VI	Welcome, Lord Somerset. What news from France?
SOMERSET	That all your interest in those territories Is utterly bereft you; all is lost.
KING HENRY VI	Cold news, Lord Somerset: but God's will be done!
YORK	[*Aside*] Cold news for me; for I had hope of France As firmly as I hope for fertile England. Thus are my blossoms blasted in the bud And caterpillars eat my leaves away; But I will remedy this gear ere long, Or sell my title for a glorious grave.

Enter GLOUCESTER

GLOUCESTER	All happiness unto my lord the king! Pardon, my liege, that I have stay'd so long.

SUFFOLK   Nay, Gloucester, know that thou art come
          too soon,
          Unless thou wert more loyal than
          thou art:
          I do arrest thee of high treason here.

GLOUCESTER   Well, Suffolk, thou shalt not see me blush
          Nor change my countenance for this
          arrest:
          A heart unspotted is not easily daunted.
          The purest spring is not so free from mud
          As I am clear from treason to my
          sovereign:
          Who can accuse me? wherein am I guilty?

YORK   'Tis thought, my lord, that you took bribes
          of France,
          And, being protector, stayed the soldiers'
          pay;
          By means whereof his highness hath
          lost France.

GLOUCESTER   Is it but thought so? what are they that
          think it?
          I never robb'd the soldiers of their pay,
          Nor ever had one penny bribe from France.
          So help me God, as I have watch'd
          the night,
          Ay, night by night, in studying good
          for England,
          That doit that e'er I wrested from the king,
          Or any groat I hoarded to my use,

	Be brought against me at my trial-day!
	No; many a pound of mine own
	proper store,
	Because I would not tax the needy
	commons,
	Have I disbursed to the garrisons,
	And never ask'd for restitution.
CARDINAL	It serves you well, my lord, to say so much.
GLOUCESTER	I say no more than truth, so help me God!
YORK	In your protectorship you did devise
	Strange tortures for offenders, never
	heard of,
	That England was defamed by tyranny.
GLOUCESTER	Why, 'tis well known that, whiles I was
	protector,
	Pity was all the fault that was in me;
	For I should melt at an offender's tears,
	And lowly words were ransom for
	their fault.
	Unless it were a bloody murderer,
	Or foul felonious thief that fleeced poor
	passengers,
	I never gave them condign punishment:
	Murder indeed, that bloody sin, I tortured
	Above the felon or what trespass else.
SUFFOLK	My lord, these faults are easy, quickly
	answered:
	But mightier crimes are laid unto your
	charge,

Whereof you cannot easily purge yourself.
I do arrest you in his highness' name;
And here commit you to my lord cardinal
To keep, until your further time of trial.

KING HENRY VI   My lord of Gloucester, 'tis my special hope
That you will clear yourself from
all suspect:
My conscience tells me you are innocent.

GLOUCESTER   Ah, gracious lord, these days are
dangerous:
Virtue is choked with foul ambition
And charity chased hence by
rancour's hand;
Foul subornation is predominant
And equity exiled your highness' land.
I know their complot is to have my life,
And if my death might make this
island happy,
And prove the period of their tyranny,
I would expend it with all willingness:
But mine is made the prologue to
their play;
For thousands more, that yet suspect
no peril,
Will not conclude their plotted tragedy.
Beaufort's red sparkling eyes blab his
heart's malice,
And Suffolk's cloudy brow his stormy
hate;

Sharp Buckingham unburthens with
his tongue
The envious load that lies upon his heart;
And dogged York, that reaches at
the moon,
Whose overweening arm I have
pluck'd back,
By false accuse doth level at my life:
And you, my sovereign lady, with the rest,
Causeless have laid disgraces on my head,
And with your best endeavour have
stirr'd up
My liefest liege to be mine enemy:
Ay, all of you have laid your heads together—
Myself had notice of your conventicles—
And all to make away my guiltless life.
I shall not want false witness to
condemn me,
Nor store of treasons to augment
my guilt;
The ancient proverb will be well effected:
'A staff is quickly found to beat a dog.'

CARDINAL   My liege, his railing is intolerable:
If those that care to keep your royal
person
From treason's secret knife and
traitor's rage
Be thus upbraided, chid and rated at,
And the offender granted scope of speech,

	'Twill make them cool in zeal unto your grace.
SUFFOLK	Hath he not twit our sovereign lady here With ignominious words, though clerkly couch'd, As if she had suborned some to swear False allegations to o'erthrow his state?
QUEEN MARGARET	But I can give the loser leave to chide.
GLOUCESTER	Far truer spoke than meant: I lose, indeed; Beshrew the winners, for they play'd me false! And well such losers may have leave to speak.
BUCKINGHAM	He'll wrest the sense and hold us here all day: Lord cardinal, he is your prisoner.
CARDINAL	Sirs, take away the duke, and guard him sure.
GLOUCESTER	Ah! thus King Henry throws away his crutch Before his legs be firm to bear his body. Thus is the shepherd beaten from thy side, And wolves are gnarling who shall gnaw thee first. Ah, that my fear were false! ah, that it were! For, good King Henry, thy decay I fear.

Exit, guarded

KING HENRY VI   My lords, what to your wisdoms
seemeth best,
Do or undo, as if ourself were here.

QUEEN MARGARET   What, will your highness leave the
parliament?

KING HENRY VI   Ay, Margaret; my heart is drown'd
with grief,
Whose flood begins to flow within
mine eyes,
My body round engirt with misery,
For what's more miserable than
discontent?
Ah, uncle Humphrey! in thy face I see
The map of honour, truth and loyalty:
And yet, good Humphrey, is the hour
to come
That e'er I proved thee false or fear'd
thy faith.
What louring star now envies thy estate,
That these great lords and Margaret
our queen
Do seek subversion of thy harmless life?
Thou never didst them wrong, nor no
man wrong;
And as the butcher takes away the calf
And binds the wretch, and beats it
when it strays,

Bearing it to the bloody slaughter-house,
Even so remorseless have they borne
him hence;
And as the dam runs lowing up and down,
Looking the way her harmless young
one went,
And can do nought but wail her
darling's loss,
Even so myself bewails good
Gloucester's case
With sad unhelpful tears, and with
dimm'd eyes
Look after him and cannot do him good,
So mighty are his vowed enemies.
His fortunes I will weep; and, 'twixt
each groan
Say 'Who's a traitor? Gloucester he is none.'

Exeunt all but QUEEN MARGARET, CARDINAL,
SUFFOLK, YORK *and* SOMERSET

5. Power Corrupt

'Uncertain way of gain! But I am in
So far in blood that sin will pluck on sin'

From RICHARD III

The villainous Richard, Duke of Gloucester, has by means of murder, manipulation and treachery managed to make himself king. Once crowned, he begins to doubt the security of his position on the throne.

ACT IV, SCENE II

London. The palace. Enter KING RICHARD III, *in pomp, crowned;* BUCKINGHAM, CATESBY, *a page, and others*

KING RICHARD III	Stand all apart. Cousin of Buckingham!
BUCKINGHAM	My gracious sovereign?
KING RICHARD III	Give me thy hand.

Here he ascends his throne

Thus high, by thy advice
And thy assistance, is King Richard
seated;
But shall we wear these honours for a day?
Or shall they last, and we rejoice in them?

BUCKINGHAM	Still live they and for ever may they last!
KING RICHARD III	O Buckingham, now do I play the touch,

To try if thou be current gold indeed.
Young Edward lives: think now what I
would say.

BUCKINGHAM	Say on, my loving lord.
KING RICHARD III	Why, Buckingham, I say I would be king,
BUCKINGHAM	Why, so you are, my thrice-renowned liege.
KING RICHARD III	Ha! am I king? 'tis so: but Edward lives.
BUCKINGHAM	True, noble prince.
KING RICHARD III	O bitter consequence,

That Edward still should live! 'True, noble
prince!'

	Cousin, thou wert not wont to be
	so dull:
	Shall I be plain? I wish the bastards dead;
	And I would have it suddenly perform'd.
	What sayest thou now? speak suddenly;
	be brief.
BUCKINGHAM	Your grace may do your pleasure.
KING RICHARD III	Tut, tut, thou art all ice, thy kindness
	freezeth:
	Say, have I thy consent that they shall die?
BUCKINGHAM	Give me some little breath, some pause,
	my lord
	Before I positively speak in this:
	I will resolve you herein presently.

Exit

CATESBY	[*Aside to a stander-by*]
	The king is angry: see, he gnaws his lip.
KING RICHARD III	I will converse with iron-witted fools
	And unrespective boys: none are for me
	That look into me with considerate eyes:
	High-reaching Buckingham grows
	circumspect.
	Boy!
Page	My lord?
KING RICHARD III	Know'st thou not any whom
	corrupting gold
	Would tempt unto a close exploit
	of death?

Page   My lord, I know a discontented
            gentleman,
            Whose humble means match not his
            haughty mind:
            Gold were as good as twenty orators,
            And will, no doubt, tempt him to any
            thing.

KING RICHARD III   What is his name?

Page   His name, my lord, is Tyrrel.

KING RICHARD III   I partly know the man: go, call him hither.

Exit Page

The deep-revolving witty Buckingham
No more shall be the neighbour to my
counsels:
Hath he so long held out with me untired,
And stops he now for breath?

Enter STANLEY

How now! what news with you?

STANLEY   My lord, I hear the Marquis Dorset's fled
            To Richmond, in those parts beyond the
            sea
            Where he abides.

Stands apart

KING RICHARD III   Catesby!

CATESBY   My lord?

KING RICHARD III   Rumour it abroad

That Anne, my wife, is sick and like to die:
I will take order for her keeping close.
Inquire me out some mean-born
gentleman,
Whom I will marry straight to Clarence'
daughter:
The boy is foolish, and I fear not him.
Look, how thou dream'st! I say again,
give out
That Anne my wife is sick and like to die:
About it; for it stands me much upon,
To stop all hopes whose growth may
damage me.

Exit CATESBY

I must be married to my brother's
daughter,
Or else my kingdom stands on brittle glass.
Murder her brothers, and then marry her!
Uncertain way of gain! But I am in
So far in blood that sin will pluck on sin:
Tear-falling pity dwells not in this eye.

Re-enter Page, with TYRREL

Is thy name Tyrrel?

TYRREL   James Tyrrel, and your most obedient
                   subject.

KING RICHARD III   Art thou, indeed?

TYRREL   Prove me, my gracious sovereign.

KING RICHARD III	Darest thou resolve to kill a friend of mine?
TYRREL	Ay, my lord;
	But I had rather kill two enemies.
KING RICHARD III	Why, there thou hast it: two deep enemies,
	Foes to my rest and my sweet sleep's disturbers
	Are they that I would have thee deal upon:
	Tyrrel, I mean those bastards in the Tower.
TYRREL	Let me have open means to come to them,
	And soon I'll rid you from the fear of them.
KING RICHARD III	Thou sing'st sweet music. Hark, come hither, Tyrrel.
	Go, by this token: rise, and lend thine ear:

Whispers

	There is no more but so: say it is done,
	And I will love thee, and prefer thee too.
TYRREL	'Tis done, my gracious lord.
KING RICHARD III	Shall we hear from thee, Tyrrel, ere we sleep?
TYRREL	Ye shall, my Lord.

Exit

Re-enter BUCKINGHAM

BUCKINGHAM	My Lord, I have consider'd in my mind
	The late demand that you did sound me in.
KING RICHARD III	Well, let that pass. Dorset is fled to Richmond.

BUCKINGHAM	I hear that news, my lord.
KING RICHARD III	Stanley, he is your wife's son. Well, look to it.
BUCKINGHAM	My lord, I claim the gift, my due by promise,
	For which your honour and your faith is pawn'd:
	The earldom of Hereford and the moveables
	The which you promised I should possess.
KING RICHARD III	Stanley, look to your wife; if she convey
	Letters to Richmond, you shall answer it.
BUCKINGHAM	What says your highness to my just demand?
KING RICHARD III	As I remember, Henry the Sixth
	Did prophesy that Richmond should be king,
	When Richmond was a little peevish boy.
	A king, perhaps, perhaps,—
BUCKINGHAM	My lord!
KING RICHARD III	How chance the prophet could not at that time
	Have told me, I being by, that I should kill him?
BUCKINGHAM	My lord, your promise for the earldom—
KING RICHARD III	Richmond! When last I was at Exeter,
	The mayor in courtesy show'd me the castle,
	And call'd it Rougemont: at which name I started,

Because a bard of Ireland told me once
I should not live long after I saw
Richmond.

KING RICHARD III   Ay, what's o'clock?

BUCKINGHAM   My Lord!

KING RICHARD III   Ay, what's o'clock?

BUCKINGHAM   I am thus bold to put your grace in mind
Of what you promised me.

KING RICHARD III   Well, but what's o'clock?

BUCKINGHAM   Upon the stroke of ten.

KING RICHARD III   Well, let it strike.

BUCKINGHAM   Why let it strike?

KING RICHARD III   Because that, like a Jack, thou keep'st the stroke
Betwixt thy begging and my meditation.
I am not in the giving vein to-day.

BUCKINGHAM   Why, then resolve me whether you will or no.

KING RICHARD III   Tut, tut,
Thou troublest me; am not in the vein.

Exeunt all but BUCKINGHAM

BUCKINGHAM   Is it even so? rewards he my true service
With such deep contempt? Made I him king for this?
O, let me think on Hastings, and be gone
To Brecknock, while my fearful head is on!

Exit

6. Tyranny

'. . .I'll not call you tyrant;
'But this most cruel usage of your queen,
Not able to produce more accusation
Than your own weak-hinged fancy,
something savours
Of tyranny . . .'

FROM A WINTER'S TALE

*King Leontes has, without discernible cause or evidence,
accused his wife Hermione of infidelity and declared her
new baby illegitimate. Antigonus is a courtier, Paulina is
his wife and a friend to Hermione.*

ACT II, SCENE III

Enter LEONTES, ANTIGONUS,
Lords, and Servants

LEONTES   Nor night nor day no rest: it is but weakness
                     To bear the matter thus; mere weakness. If
                     The cause were not in being,—part o' the
                     cause,
                     She the adulteress; for the harlot king
                     Is quite beyond mine arm, out of the blank
                     And level of my brain, plot-proof; but she
                     I can hook to me: say that she were gone,
                     Given to the fire, a moiety of my rest
                     Might come to me again. Who's there?

FIRST SERVANT   My lord?

LEONTES   How does the boy?

FIRST SERVANT   He took good rest to-night;
                     'Tis hoped his sickness is discharged.

LEONTES   To see his nobleness!
                     Conceiving the dishonour of his mother,
                     He straight declined, droop'd, took it deeply,
                     Fasten'd and fix'd the shame on't in himself,
                     Threw off his spirit, his appetite, his sleep,
                     And downright languish'd. Leave me
                     solely: go,
                     See how he fares.

Exit Servant

> Fie, fie! no thought of him:
> The thought of my revenges that way
> Recoil upon me: in himself too mighty,
> And in his parties, his alliance; let him be
> Until a time may serve: for present vengeance,
> Take it on her. Camillo and Polixenes
> Laugh at me, make their pastime at my sorrow:
> They should not laugh if I could reach them,
>   nor
> Shall she within my power.

Enter PAULINA, *carrying a baby*

FIRST LORD	You must not enter.
PAULINA	Nay, rather, good my lords, be second to me:
	Fear you his tyrannous passion more, alas,
	Than the queen's life? a gracious
	innocent soul,
	More free than he is jealous.
ANTIGONUS	That's enough.
SECOND SERVANT	Madam, he hath not slept tonight;
	commanded
	None should come at him.
PAULINA	Not so hot, good sir:
	I come to bring him sleep. 'Tis such as you,
	That creep like shadows by him and do sigh
	At each his needless heavings, such as you
	Nourish the cause of his awaking: I

	Do come with words as medicinal as true,

Do come with words as medicinal as true,
Honest as either, to purge him of that humour
That presses him from sleep.

LEONTES   What noise there, ho?

PAULINA   No noise, my lord; but needful conference
About some gossips for your highness.

LEONTES   How!
Away with that audacious lady! Antigonus,
I charged thee that she should not come
about me:
I knew she would.

ANTIGONUS   I told her so, my lord,
On your displeasure's peril and on mine,
She should not visit you.

LEONTES   What, canst not rule her?

PAULINA   From all dishonesty he can: in this,
Unless he take the course that you have done,
Commit me for committing honour, trust it,
He shall not rule me.

ANTIGONUS   La you now, you hear:
When she will take the rein I let her run;
But she'll not stumble.

PAULINA   Good my liege, I come;
And, I beseech you, hear me, who profess
Myself your loyal servant, your physician,
Your most obedient counsellor, yet that dare
Less appear so in comforting your evils,
Than such as most seem yours: I say, I come
From your good queen.

LEONTES	Good queen!
PAULINA	Good queen, my lord,
	Good queen; I say good queen;
	And would by combat make her good, so were I
	A man, the worst about you.
LEONTES	Force her hence.
PAULINA	Let him that makes but trifles of his eyes
	First hand me: on mine own accord I'll off;
	But first I'll do my errand. The good queen,
	For she is good, hath brought you forth a daughter;
	Here 'tis; commends it to your blessing.

Laying down the child

LEONTES	Out!
	A mankind witch! Hence with her, out o' door:
	A most intelligencing bawd!
PAULINA	Not so:
	I am as ignorant in that as you
	In so entitling me, and no less honest
	Than you are mad; which is enough, I'll warrant,
	As this world goes, to pass for honest.
LEONTES	Traitors!
	Will you not push her out? Give her the bastard.
	Thou dotard! thou art woman-tired, unroosted
	By thy dame Partlet here. Take up the bastard;
	Take't up, I say; give't to thy crone.
PAULINA	For ever
	Unvenerable be thy hands, if thou

	Takest up the princess by that forced baseness
	Which he has put upon't!
LEONTES	He dreads his wife.
PAULINA	So I would you did; then 'twere past all doubt
	You'ld call your children yours.
LEONTES	A nest of traitors!
ANTIGONUS	I am none, by this good light.
PAULINA	Nor I, nor any
	But one that's here, and that's himself, for he
	The sacred honour of himself, his queen's,
	His hopeful son's, his babe's, betrays to slander,
	Whose sting is sharper than the sword's;
	and will not—
	For, as the case now stands, it is a curse
	He cannot be compell'd to't—once remove
	The root of his opinion, which is rotten
	As ever oak or stone was sound.
LEONTES	A callat
	Of boundless tongue, who late hath beat her
	husband
	And now baits me! This brat is none of mine;
	It is the issue of Polixenes:
	Hence with it, and together with the dam
	Commit them to the fire!
PAULINA	It is yours;
	And, might we lay the old proverb to your charge,
	So like you, 'tis the worse. Behold, my lords,
	Although the print be little, the whole matter
	And copy of the father, eye, nose, lip,

	The trick of's frown, his forehead, nay, the valley,
	The pretty dimples of his chin and cheek,
	His smiles,
	The very mould and frame of hand, nail, finger:
	And thou, good goddess Nature, which hast made it
	So like to him that got it, if thou hast
	The ordering of the mind too, 'mongst all colours
	No yellow in't, lest she suspect, as he does,
	Her children not her husband's!
LEONTES	A gross hag
	And, lozel, thou art worthy to be hang'd,
	That wilt not stay her tongue.
ANTIGONUS	Hang all the husbands
	That cannot do that feat, you'll leave yourself
	Hardly one subject.
LEONTES	Once more, take her hence.
PAULINA	A most unworthy and unnatural lord
	Can do no more.
LEONTES	I'll ha' thee burnt.
PAULINA	I care not:
	It is an heretic that makes the fire,
	Not she which burns in't. I'll not call you tyrant;
	But this most cruel usage of your queen,
	Not able to produce more accusation
	Than your own weak-hinged fancy, something savours
	Of tyranny and will ignoble make you,
	Yea, scandalous to the world.

LEONTES   On your allegiance,
            Out of the chamber with her! Were I a tyrant,
            Where were her life? she durst not call me so,
            If she did know me one. Away with her!

PAULINA   I pray you, do not push me; I'll be gone.
            Look to your babe, my lord; 'tis yours:
            Jove send her
            A better guiding spirit! What needs these
            hands?
            You, that are thus so tender o'er his follies,
            Will never do him good, not one of you.
            So, so: farewell; we are gone.

                        Exit

LEONTES   Thou, traitor, hast set on thy wife to this.
            My child? away with't! Even thou, that hast
            A heart so tender o'er it, take it hence
            And see it instantly consumed with fire;
            Even thou and none but thou. Take it up straight:
            Within this hour bring me word 'tis done,
            And by good testimony, or I'll seize thy life,
            With what thou else call'st thine. If thou refuse
            And wilt encounter with my wrath, say so;
            The bastard brains with these my proper hands
            Shall I dash out. Go, take it to the fire;
            For thou set'st on thy wife.

ANTIGONUS   I did not, sir:
            These lords, my noble fellows, if they please,
            Can clear me in't.

LORDS   We can: my royal liege,
            He is not guilty of her coming hither.

LEONTES   You're liars all.

FIRST LORD Beseech your highness, give us better credit:
            We have always truly served you, and
            beseech you
            So to esteem of us, and on our knees we beg,
            As recompense of our dear services
            Past and to come, that you do change this purpose,
            Which being so horrible, so bloody, must
            Lead on to some foul issue: we all kneel.

LEONTES   I am a feather for each wind that blows:
            Shall I live on to see this bastard kneel
            And call me father? better burn it now
            Than curse it then. But be it; let it live.
            It shall not neither. You, sir, come you hither;
            You that have been so tenderly officious
            With Lady Margery, your midwife there,
            To save this bastard's life,—for 'tis a bastard,
            So sure as this beard's grey,
            —what will you adventure
            To save this brat's life?

ANTIGONUS   Any thing, my lord,
            That my ability may undergo
            And nobleness impose: at least thus much:
            I'll pawn the little blood which I have left
            To save the innocent: any thing possible.

LEONTES   It shall be possible. Swear by this sword
            Thou wilt perform my bidding.

ANTIGONUS I will, my lord.

LEONTES Mark and perform it, see'st thou! for the fail
Of any point in't shall not only be
Death to thyself but to thy lewd-tongued wife,
Whom for this time we pardon. We enjoin thee,
As thou art liege-man to us, that thou carry
This female bastard hence and that thou bear it
To some remote and desert place quite out
Of our dominions, and that there thou leave it,
Without more mercy, to its own protection
And favour of the climate. As by strange fortune
It came to us, I do in justice charge thee,
On thy soul's peril and thy body's torture,
That thou commend it strangely to some place
Where chance may nurse or end it. Take it up.

ANTIGONUS I swear to do this, though a present death
Had been more merciful. Come on, poor babe:
Some powerful spirit instruct the kites and
ravens
To be thy nurses! Wolves and bears, they say,
Casting their savageness aside, have done
Like offices of pity. Sir, be prosperous
In more than this deed does require! And blessing
Against this cruelty fight on thy side,
Poor thing, condemn'd to loss!

Exit with the child

7. Subjection

'Such duty as the subject owes the prince
Even such a woman oweth to her husband'

Baptista's daughter Katharina has a widespread reputation as a bad-tempered, unmanageable 'shrew'. Her pretty sister Bianca is docility itself, but none of her suitors can hope to win her and her plentiful dowry unless Katharina is married first. Petruchio takes on the challenge of 'taming' Kate, and marries her, and by the end of the play Bianca is married to Lucentio and one of her other suitors, Hortensio, has married a rich widow. Here, Petruchio suggests a bet with the other men to prove which of their wives is most obedient.

ACT V, SCENE II

BAPTISTA	Now, in good sadness, son Petruchio,
	I think thou hast the veriest shrew of all.
PETRUCHIO	Well, I say no: and therefore for assurance
	Let's each one send unto his wife;
	And he whose wife is most obedient
	To come at first when he doth send for her,
	Shall win the wager which we will propose.
HORTENSIO	Content. What is the wager?
LUCENTIO	Twenty crowns.
PETRUCHIO	Twenty crowns!
	I'll venture so much of my hawk or hound,
	But twenty times so much upon my wife.
LUCENTIO	A hundred then.
HORTENSIO	Content.
PETRUCHIO	A match! 'tis done.
HORTENSIO	Who shall begin?
LUCENTIO	That will I.
	Go, Biondello, bid your mistress come to me.
BIONDELLO	I go.

Exit

BAPTISTA	Son, I'll be your half, Bianca comes.
LUCENTIO	I'll have no halves; I'll bear it all myself.

Re-enter BIONDELLO

How now! What news?

BIONDELLO   Sir, my mistress sends you word
            That she is busy and she cannot come.

PETRUCHIO   How! She is busy and she cannot come!
            Is that an answer?

GREMIO   Ay, and a kind one too:
            Pray God, sir, your wife send you not a worse.

PETRUCHIO   I hope better.

HORTENSIO   Sirrah Biondello, go and entreat my wife
            To come to me forthwith.

Exit BIONDELLO

PETRUCHIO   O, ho! Entreat her!
            Nay, then she must needs come.

HORTENSIO   I am afraid, sir,
            Do what you can, yours will not be entreated.

Re-enter BIONDELLO

            Now, where's my wife?

BIONDELLO   She says you have some goodly jest in hand:
            She will not come: she bids you come to her.

PETRUCHIO   Worse and worse; she will not come! O vile,
            Intolerable, not to be endured!
            Sirrah Grumio, go to your mistress;
            Say, I command her to come to me.

Exit GRUMIO

HORTENSIO   I know her answer.

PETRUCHIO   What?

HORTENSIO   She will not.

PETRUCHIO	The fouler fortune mine, and there an end.
BAPTISTA	Now, by my holidame, here comes Katharina!

Re-enter KATHARINA

KATHARINA	What is your will, sir, that you send for me?
PETRUCHIO	Where is your sister, and Hortensio's wife?
KATHARINA	They sit conferring by the parlour fire.
PETRUCHIO	Go fetch them hither: if they deny to come, Swinge me them soundly forth unto their husbands: Away, I say, and bring them hither straight.

Exit KATHARINA

LUCENTIO	Here is a wonder, if you talk of a wonder.
HORTENSIO	And so it is: I wonder what it bodes.
PETRUCHIO	Marry, peace it bodes, and love and quiet life, And awful rule and right supremacy; And, to be short, what not, that's sweet and happy?
BAPTISTA	Now, fair befall thee, good Petruchio! The wager thou hast won; and I will add Unto their losses twenty thousand crowns; Another dowry to another daughter, For she is changed, as she had never been.
PETRUCHIO	Nay, I will win my wager better yet And show more sign of her obedience, Her new-built virtue and obedience.

See where she comes and brings your
froward wives
As prisoners to her womanly persuasion.

Re-enter KATHARINA,
with BIANCA *and the* WIDOW

Katharina, that cap of yours becomes you not:
Off with that bauble, throw it under-foot.

WIDOW   Lord, let me never have a cause to sigh,
Till I be brought to such a silly pass!

BIANCA   Fie! What a foolish duty call you this?

LUCENTIO I would your duty were as foolish too:
The wisdom of your duty, fair Bianca,
Hath cost me a hundred crowns since
supper-time.

BIANCA   The more fool you, for laying on my duty.

PETRUCHIO Katharina, I charge thee, tell these headstrong
women
What duty they do owe their lords and
husbands.

WIDOW   Come, come, you're mocking: we will have no
telling.

PETRUCHIO Come on, I say; and first begin with her.

WIDOW   She shall not.

PETRUCHIO I say she shall: and first begin with her.

KATHARINA Fie, fie! Unknit that threatening unkind brow,
And dart not scornful glances from those eyes,
To wound thy lord, thy king, thy governor:
It blots thy beauty as frosts do bite the meads,

Confounds thy fame as whirlwinds shake
fair buds,
And in no sense is meet or amiable.
A woman moved is like a fountain troubled,
Muddy, ill-seeming, thick, bereft of beauty;
And while it is so, none so dry or thirsty
Will deign to sip or touch one drop of it.
Thy husband is thy lord, thy life, thy keeper,
Thy head, thy sovereign; one that cares for thee,
And for thy maintenance commits his body
To painful labour both by sea and land,
To watch the night in storms, the day in cold,
Whilst thou liest warm at home, secure and safe;
And craves no other tribute at thy hands
But love, fair looks and true obedience;
Too little payment for so great a debt.
Such duty as the subject owes the prince
Even such a woman oweth to her husband;
And when she is froward, peevish, sullen, sour,
And not obedient to his honest will,
What is she but a foul contending rebel
And graceless traitor to her loving lord?
I am ashamed that women are so simple
To offer war where they should kneel for peace;
Or seek for rule, supremacy and sway,
When they are bound to serve, love and obey.
Why are our bodies soft and weak and smooth,
Unapt to toil and trouble in the world,
But that our soft conditions and our hearts

Should well agree with our external parts?
Come, come, you froward and unable worms!
My mind hath been as big as one of yours,
My heart as great, my reason haply more,
To bandy word for word and frown for frown;
But now I see our lances are but straws,
Our strength as weak, our weakness past
compare,
That seeming to be most which we indeed
least are.
Then vail your stomachs, for it is no boot,
And place your hands below your husband's foot:
In token of which duty, if he please,
My hand is ready; may it do him ease.

PETRUCHIO   Why, there's a wench! Come on, and
kiss me, Kate.

LUCENTIO   Well, go thy ways, old lad; for thou shalt ha't.

VINCENTIO   'Tis a good hearing when children are toward.

LUCENTIO   But a harsh hearing when women are froward.

PETRUCHIO   Come, Kate, we'll to bed.
We three are married, but you two are sped.

To LUCENTIO

'Twas I won the wager, though you hit the white;
And, being a winner, God give you good night!

Exeunt PETRUCHIO *and* KATHARINA

8. Mind Control

'Though I am bound to every act of duty,
I am not bound to that all slaves are free to.'

From OTHELLO

Othello is an honoured general who has recently married
the young and virtuous Desdemona. Iago, a soldier in Oth-
ello's command, secretly loathes his superior and seeks to
ruin his happiness and reputation. He skilfully manipu-
lates Othello, suggesting that his new wife is having an
affair with another soldier, Cassio. Emilia is Desdemona's
maid, and Iago's wife.

ACT III, SCENE III

IAGO	My noble lord—
OTHELLO	What dost thou say, Iago?
IAGO	Did Michael Cassio, when you woo'd my lady,
	Know of your love?
OTHELLO	He did, from first to last: why dost thou ask?
IAGO	But for a satisfaction of my thought;
	No further harm.
OTHELLO	Why of thy thought, Iago?
IAGO	I did not think he had been acquainted with her.
OTHELLO	O, yes; and went between us very oft.
IAGO	Indeed!
OTHELLO	Indeed! ay, indeed: discern'st thou aught in that?
	Is he not honest?
IAGO	Honest, my lord!
OTHELLO	Honest! ay, honest.
IAGO	My lord, for aught I know.
OTHELLO	What dost thou think?
IAGO	Think, my lord!
OTHELLO	Think, my lord!
	By heaven, he echoes me,
	As if there were some monster in his thought
	Too hideous to be shown. Thou dost mean
	something:
	I heard thee say even now, thou likedst not that,
	When Cassio left my wife: what didst not like?
	And when I told thee he was of my counsel

In my whole course of wooing, thou criedst
'Indeed!'
And didst contract and purse thy brow together,
As if thou then hadst shut up in thy brain
Some horrible conceit: if thou dost love me,
Show me thy thought.

IAGO   My lord, you know I love you.

OTHELLO   I think thou dost;
And, for I know thou'rt full of love and honesty,
And weigh'st thy words before thou givest them
breath,
Therefore these stops of thine fright me
the more:
For such things in a false disloyal knave
Are tricks of custom, but in a man that's just
They are close delations, working from the heart
That passion cannot rule.

IAGO   For Michael Cassio,
I dare be sworn I think that he is honest.

OTHELLO   I think so too.

IAGO   Men should be what they seem;
Or those that be not, would they might seem none!

OTHELLO   Certain, men should be what they seem.

IAGO   Why, then, I think Cassio's an honest man.

OTHELLO   Nay, yet there's more in this:
I prithee, speak to me as to thy thinkings,
As thou dost ruminate, and give thy worst of
thoughts
The worst of words.

IAGO   Good my lord, pardon me:
        Though I am bound to every act of duty,
        I am not bound to that all slaves are free to.
        Utter my thoughts? Why, say they are vile
        and false;
        As where's that palace whereinto foul things
        Sometimes intrude not? who has a breast
        so pure,
        But some uncleanly apprehensions
        Keep leets and law-days and in session sit
        With meditations lawful?

OTHELLO Thou dost conspire against thy friend, Iago,
        If thou but think'st him wrong'd and makest
        his ear
        A stranger to thy thoughts.

IAGO   I do beseech you—
        Though I perchance am vicious in my guess,
        As, I confess, it is my nature's plague
        To spy into abuses, and oft my jealousy
        Shapes faults that are not—that your wisdom yet,
        From one that so imperfectly conceits,
        Would take no notice, nor build yourself a trouble
        Out of his scattering and unsure observance.
        It were not for your quiet nor your good,
        Nor for my manhood, honesty, or wisdom,
        To let you know my thoughts.

OTHELLO What dost thou mean?

IAGO   Good name in man and woman, dear my lord,
        Is the immediate jewel of their souls:

               Who steals my purse steals trash; 'tis
               something, nothing;
               'Twas mine, 'tis his, and has been slave to
               thousands:
               But he that filches from me my good name
               Robs me of that which not enriches him
               And makes me poor indeed.

OTHELLO   By heaven, I'll know thy thoughts.

IAGO   You cannot, if my heart were in your hand;
               Nor shall not, whilst 'tis in my custody.

OTHELLO   Ha!

IAGO   O, beware, my lord, of jealousy;
               It is the green-eyed monster which doth mock
               The meat it feeds on; that cuckold lives in bliss
               Who, certain of his fate, loves not his wronger;
               But, O, what damned minutes tells he o'er
               Who dotes, yet doubts, suspects, yet strongly
               loves!

OTHELLO   O misery!

IAGO   Poor and content is rich and rich enough,
               But riches fineless is as poor as winter
               To him that ever fears he shall be poor.
               Good heaven, the souls of all my tribe defend
               From jealousy!

OTHELLO   Why, why is this?
               Think'st thou I'ld make a life of jealousy,
               To follow still the changes of the moon
               With fresh suspicions? No; to be once in doubt
               Is once to be resolved: exchange me for a goat,

When I shall turn the business of my soul
To such exsufflicate and blown surmises,
Matching thy inference. 'Tis not to make
me jealous
To say my wife is fair, feeds well, loves
company,
Is free of speech, sings, plays and dances well;
Where virtue is, these are more virtuous:
Nor from mine own weak merits will I draw
The smallest fear or doubt of her revolt;
For she had eyes, and chose me. No, Iago;
I'll see before I doubt; when I doubt, prove;
And on the proof, there is no more but this,—
Away at once with love or jealousy!

IAGO   I am glad of it; for now I shall have reason
To show the love and duty that I bear you
With franker spirit: therefore, as I am bound,
Receive it from me. I speak not yet of proof.
Look to your wife; observe her well
with Cassio;
Wear your eye thus, not jealous nor secure:
I would not have your free and noble nature,
Out of self-bounty, be abused; look to't:
I know our country disposition well;
In Venice they do let heaven see the pranks
They dare not show their husbands; their best
conscience
Is not to leave't undone, but keep't unknown.

OTHELLO   Dost thou say so?

IAGO	She did deceive her father, marrying you;
	And when she seem'd to shake and fear your looks,
	She loved them most.
OTHELLO	And so she did.
IAGO	Why, go to then;
	She that, so young, could give out such a seeming,
	To seal her father's eyes up close as oak—
	He thought 'twas witchcraft—but I am much to blame;
	I humbly do beseech you of your pardon
	For too much loving you.
OTHELLO	I am bound to thee for ever.
IAGO	I see this hath a little dash'd your spirits.
OTHELLO	Not a jot, not a jot.
IAGO	I' faith, I fear it has.
	I hope you will consider what is spoke
	Comes from my love. But I do see you're moved:
	I am to pray you not to strain my speech
	To grosser issues nor to larger reach
	Than to suspicion.
OTHELLO	I will not.
IAGO	Should you do so, my lord,
	My speech should fall into such vile success
	As my thoughts aim not at. Cassio's my worthy friend—
	My lord, I see you're moved.
OTHELLO	No, not much moved:

	I do not think but Desdemona's honest.
IAGO	Long live she so! and long live you to think so!
OTHELLO	And yet, how nature erring from itself,—
IAGO	Ay, there's the point: as—to be bold with you—

Not to affect many proposed matches
Of her own clime, complexion, and degree,
Whereto we see in all things nature tends—
Foh! one may smell in such a will most rank,
Foul disproportion, thoughts unnatural.
But pardon me; I do not in position
Distinctly speak of her; though I may fear
Her will, recoiling to her better judgment,
May fall to match you with her country forms
And happily repent.

| OTHELLO | Farewell, farewell: |

If more thou dost perceive, let me know more;
Set on thy wife to observe: leave me, Iago:

| IAGO | [*Going*] My lord, I take my leave. |

| OTHELLO | Why did I marry? This honest creature doubtless |

Sees and knows more, much more, than he
unfolds.

| IAGO | [*Returning*] My lord, I would I might entreat your honour |

To scan this thing no further; leave it to time:
Though it be fit that Cassio have his place,
For sure, he fills it up with great ability,
Yet, if you please to hold him off awhile,
You shall by that perceive him and his means:
Note, if your lady strain his entertainment

With any strong or vehement importunity;
Much will be seen in that. In the mean time,
Let me be thought too busy in my fears—
As worthy cause I have to fear I am—
And hold her free, I do beseech your honour.

OTHELLO   Fear not my government.

IAGO   I once more take my leave.

Exit

OTHELLO   This fellow's of exceeding honesty,
And knows all qualities, with a learned spirit,
Of human dealings. If I do prove her haggard,
Though that her jesses were my dear
heartstrings,
I'ld whistle her off and let her down the wind,
To prey at fortune. Haply, for I am black
And have not those soft parts of conversation
That chamberers have, or for I am declined
Into the vale of years,—yet that's not much—
She's gone, I am abused; and my relief
Must be to loathe her. O curse of marriage,
That we can call these delicate creatures ours,
And not their appetites! I had rather be a toad,
And live upon the vapour of a dungeon,
Than keep a corner in the thing I love
For others' uses. Yet, 'tis the plague of great
ones;
Prerogatived are they less than the base;
'Tis destiny unshunnable, like death:

Even then this forked plague is fated to us
When we do quicken. Desdemona comes:

Re-enter DESDEMONA *and* EMILIA

If she be false, O, then heaven mocks itself!
I'll not believe't.

DESDEMONA How now, my dear Othello!
Your dinner, and the generous islanders
By you invited, do attend your presence.

OTHELLO I am to blame.

DESDEMONA Why do you speak so faintly?
Are you not well?

OTHELLO I have a pain upon my forehead here.

DESDEMONA 'Faith, that's with watching; 'twill away again:
Let me but bind it hard, within this hour
It will be well.

OTHELLO Your napkin is too little:

He puts the handkerchief from him; and it drops

Let it alone. Come, I'll go in with you.

DESDEMONA I am very sorry that you are not well.

Exeunt OTHELLO *and* DESDEMONA

EMILIA I am glad I have found this napkin:
This was her first remembrance from the Moor:
My wayward husband hath a hundred times
Woo'd me to steal it; but she so loves the token,
For he conjured her she should ever keep it,
That she reserves it evermore about her

To kiss and talk to. I'll have the work ta'en out,
And give't Iago: what he will do with it
Heaven knows, not I;
I nothing but to please his fantasy.

Re-enter Iago

IAGO	How now! what do you here alone?
EMILIA	Do not you chide; I have a thing for you.
IAGO	A thing for me? it is a common thing—
EMILIA	Ha!
IAGO	To have a foolish wife.
EMILIA	O, is that all? What will you give me now For the same handkerchief?
IAGO	What handkerchief?
EMILIA	What handkerchief? Why, that the Moor first gave to Desdemona; That which so often you did bid me steal.
IAGO	Hast stol'n it from her?
EMILIA	No, 'faith; she let it drop by negligence. And, to the advantage, I, being here, took't up. Look, here it is.
IAGO	A good wench; give it me.
EMILIA	What will you do with 't, that you have been so earnest To have me filch it?
IAGO	[*Snatching it*] Why, what's that to you?
EMILIA	If it be not for some purpose of import, Give't me again: poor lady, she'll run mad When she shall lack it.

IAGO   Be not acknown on 't; I have use for it.
               Go, leave me.

Exit EMILIA

I will in Cassio's lodging lose this napkin,
And let him find it. Trifles light as air
Are to the jealous confirmations strong
As proofs of holy writ: this may do something.
The Moor already changes with my poison:
Dangerous conceits are, in their natures,
poisons,
Which at the first are scarce found to distaste,
But with a little act upon the blood
Burn like the mines of sulphur. I did say so:
Look, where he comes!

Re-enter OTHELLO

Not poppy, nor mandragora,
Nor all the drowsy syrups of the world,
Shall ever medicine thee to that sweet sleep
Which thou owedst yesterday.

OTHELLO   Ha! ha! false to me?
IAGO   Why, how now, general! no more of that.
OTHELLO   Avaunt! be gone! thou hast set me on the rack:
               I swear 'tis better to be much abused
               Than but to know't a little.
IAGO   How now, my lord!
OTHELLO   What sense had I of her stol'n hours of lust?
               I saw't not, thought it not, it harm'd not me:

I slept the next night well, was free and merry;
I found not Cassio's kisses on her lips:
He that is robb'd, not wanting what is stol'n,
Let him not know't, and he's not robb'd at all.

IAGO   I am sorry to hear this.

OTHELLO   I had been happy, if the general camp,
Pioners and all, had tasted her sweet body,
So I had nothing known. O, now, for ever
Farewell the tranquil mind! farewell content!
Farewell the plumed troop, and the big wars,
That make ambition virtue! O, farewell!
Farewell the neighing steed, and the shrill trump,
The spirit-stirring drum, the ear-piercing fife,
The royal banner, and all quality,
Pride, pomp and circumstance of glorious war!
And, O you mortal engines, whose rude throats
The immortal Jove's dead clamours counterfeit,
Farewell! Othello's occupation's gone!

IAGO   Is't possible, my lord?

OTHELLO   Villain, be sure thou prove my love a whore,
Be sure of it; give me the ocular proof:
Or by the worth of man's eternal soul,
Thou hadst been better have been born a dog
Than answer my waked wrath!

IAGO   Is't come to this?

OTHELLO   Make me to see't; or, at the least, so prove it,
That the probation bear no hinge nor loop
To hang a doubt on; or woe upon thy life!

IAGO   My noble lord,—

OTHELLO   If thou dost slander her and torture me,
            Never pray more; abandon all remorse;
            On horror's head horrors accumulate;
            Do deeds to make heaven weep, all earth amazed;
            For nothing canst thou to damnation add
            Greater than that.

IAGO   O grace! O heaven forgive me!
            Are you a man? have you a soul or sense?
            God be wi' you; take mine office.
            O wretched fool.
            That livest to make thine honesty a vice!
            O monstrous world! Take note, take note,
            O world,
            To be direct and honest is not safe.
            I thank you for this profit; and from hence
            I'll love no friend, sith love breeds such offence.

OTHELLO   Nay, stay: thou shouldst be honest.

IAGO   I should be wise, for honesty's a fool
            And loses that it works for.

OTHELLO   By the world,
            I think my wife be honest and think she is not;
            I think that thou art just and think thou art not.
            I'll have some proof. My name, that was as
            fresh
            As Dian's visage, is now begrimed and black
            As mine own face. If there be cords, or knives,
            Poison, or fire, or suffocating streams,
            I'll not endure it. Would I were satisfied!

IAGO   I see, sir, you are eaten up with passion:

I do repent me that I put it to you.
You would be satisfied?

OTHELLO   Would! nay, I will.

IAGO   And may: but, how? how satisfied, my lord?
Would you, the supervisor, grossly gape on—
Behold her topp'd?

OTHELLO   Death and damnation! O!

IAGO   It were a tedious difficulty, I think,
To bring them to that prospect: damn
them then,
If ever mortal eyes do see them bolster
More than their own! What then? how then?
What shall I say? Where's satisfaction?
It is impossible you should see this,
Were they as prime as goats, as hot as monkeys,
As salt as wolves in pride, and fools as gross
As ignorance made drunk. But yet, I say,
If imputation and strong circumstances,
Which lead directly to the door of truth,
Will give you satisfaction, you may have't.

OTHELLO   Give me a living reason she's disloyal.

IAGO   I do not like the office:
But, sith I am enter'd in this cause so far,
Prick'd to't by foolish honesty and love,
I will go on. I lay with Cassio lately;
And, being troubled with a raging tooth,
I could not sleep.
There are a kind of men so loose of soul,
That in their sleeps will mutter their affairs:

One of this kind is Cassio:
In sleep I heard him say 'Sweet Desdemona,
Let us be wary, let us hide our loves;'
And then, sir, would he gripe and wring my hand,
Cry 'O sweet creature!' and then kiss me hard,
As if he pluck'd up kisses by the roots
That grew upon my lips: then laid his leg
Over my thigh, and sigh'd, and kiss'd; and then
Cried 'Cursed fate that gave thee to the Moor!'

OTHELLO   O monstrous! monstrous!

IAGO   Nay, this was but his dream.

OTHELLO   But this denoted a foregone conclusion:
'Tis a shrewd doubt, though it be but a dream.

IAGO   And this may help to thicken other proofs
That do demonstrate thinly.

OTHELLO   I'll tear her all to pieces.

IAGO   Nay, but be wise: yet we see nothing done;
She may be honest yet. Tell me but this,
Have you not sometimes seen a handkerchief
Spotted with strawberries in your wife's hand?

OTHELLO   I gave her such a one; 'twas my first gift.

IAGO   I know not that; but such a handkerchief—
I am sure it was your wife's—did I to-day
See Cassio wipe his beard with.

OTHELLO   If it be that—

IAGO   If it be that, or any that was hers,
It speaks against her with the other proofs.

OTHELLO   O, that the slave had forty thousand lives!
One is too poor, too weak for my revenge.

Now do I see 'tis true. Look here, Iago;
All my fond love thus do I blow to heaven.
'Tis gone.
Arise, black vengeance, from thy hollow cell!
Yield up, O love, thy crown and hearted throne
To tyrannous hate! Swell, bosom, with thy
fraught,
For 'tis of aspics' tongues!

IAGO   Yet be content.

OTHELLO   O, blood, blood, blood!

IAGO   Patience, I say; your mind perhaps may change.

OTHELLO   Never, Iago: Like to the Pontic sea,
Whose icy current and compulsive course
Ne'er feels retiring ebb, but keeps due on
To the Propontic and the Hellespont,
Even so my bloody thoughts, with violent pace,
Shall ne'er look back, ne'er ebb to humble love,
Till that a capable and wide revenge
Swallow them up. Now, by yond marble heaven,

Kneels

In the due reverence of a sacred vow
I here engage my words.

IAGO   Do not rise yet.

Kneels

Witness, you ever-burning lights above,
You elements that clip us round about,
Witness that here Iago doth give up

The execution of his wit, hands, heart,
To wrong'd Othello's service! Let him
command,
And to obey shall be in me remorse,
What bloody business ever.

They rise

OTHELLO   I greet thy love,
Not with vain thanks, but with acceptance
bounteous,
And will upon the instant put thee to't:
Within these three days let me hear thee say
That Cassio's not alive.

IAGO   My friend is dead; 'tis done at your request:
But let her live.

OTHELLO   Damn her, lewd minx! O, damn her!
Come, go with me apart; I will withdraw,
To furnish me with some swift means of death
For the fair devil. Now art thou my lieutenant.

IAGO   I am your own for ever.

Exeunt

9. Winning Hearts and Minds

'I come not, friends, to steal away your hearts:
I am no orator, as Brutus is;
But, as you know me all, a plain blunt man,
That love my friend.'

From JULIUS CAESAR

Julius Caesar has been assassinated by a group of senators. One of the assassins, Brutus, makes a speech at Caesar's funeral to the citizens of Rome to explain that Caesar was killed in order to prevent him becoming a tyrant. Brutus then unwisely allows Mark Anthony, Caesar's closest follower, to make a public speech.

ACT III, SCENE II

FIRST CITIZEN	Stay, ho! and let us hear Mark Antony.
THIRD CITIZEN	Let him go up into the public chair;
	We'll hear him. Noble Antony, go up.
ANTONY	For Brutus' sake, I am beholding to you.

Goes into the pulpit

FOURTH CITIZEN	What does he say of Brutus?
THIRD CITIZEN	He says, for Brutus' sake,
	He finds himself beholding to us all.
FOURTH CITIZEN	'Twere best he speak no harm of Brutus here.
FIRST CITIZEN	This Caesar was a tyrant.
THIRD CITIZEN	Nay, that's certain:
	We are blest that Rome is rid of him.
SECOND CITIZEN	Peace! let us hear what Antony can say.
ANTONY	You gentle Romans,—
CITIZENS	Peace, ho! let us hear him.
ANTONY	Friends, Romans, countrymen, lend me your ears;
	I come to bury Caesar, not to praise him.
	The evil that men do lives after them;
	The good is oft interred with their bones;
	So let it be with Caesar. The noble Brutus
	Hath told you Caesar was ambitious:
	If it were so, it was a grievous fault,
	And grievously hath Caesar answer'd it.

Here, under leave of Brutus and the rest—
For Brutus is an honourable man;
So are they all, all honourable men—
Come I to speak in Caesar's funeral.
He was my friend, faithful and just to me:
But Brutus says he was ambitious;
And Brutus is an honourable man.
He hath brought many captives
home to Rome
Whose ransoms did the general coffers fill:
Did this in Caesar seem ambitious?
When that the poor have cried, Caesar
hath wept:
Ambition should be made of sterner stuff:
Yet Brutus says he was ambitious;
And Brutus is an honourable man.
You all did see that on the Lupercal
I thrice presented him a kingly crown,
Which he did thrice refuse: was this
ambition?
Yet Brutus says he was ambitious;
And, sure, he is an honourable man.
I speak not to disprove what Brutus spoke,
But here I am to speak what I do know.
You all did love him once, not
without cause:
What cause withholds you then, to mourn
for him?
O judgment! thou art fled to brutish beasts,

	And men have lost their reason.
	Bear with me;
	My heart is in the coffin there with Caesar,
	And I must pause till it come back to me.
FIRST CITIZEN	Methinks there is much reason in his sayings.
SECOND CITIZEN	If thou consider rightly of the matter, Caesar has had great wrong.
THIRD CITIZEN	Has he, masters?
	I fear there will a worse come in his place.
FOURTH CITIZEN	Mark'd ye his words? He would not take the crown;
	Therefore 'tis certain he was not ambitious.
FIRST CITIZEN	If it be found so, some will dear abide it.
SECOND CITIZEN	Poor soul! his eyes are red as fire with weeping.
THIRD CITIZEN	There's not a nobler man in Rome than Antony.
FOURTH CITIZEN	Now mark him, he begins again to speak.
ANTONY	But yesterday the word of Caesar might Have stood against the world; now lies he there.
	And none so poor to do him reverence.
	O masters, if I were disposed to stir
	Your hearts and minds to mutiny and rage,
	I should do Brutus wrong, and Cassius wrong,
	Who, you all know, are honourable men:

I will not do them wrong; I rather choose
To wrong the dead, to wrong myself
and you,
Than I will wrong such honourable men.
But here's a parchment with the seal of
Caesar;
I found it in his closet, 'tis his will:
Let but the commons hear this testament—
Which, pardon me, I do not mean to read—
And they would go and kiss dead Caesar's
wounds
And dip their napkins in his sacred blood,
Yea, beg a hair of him for memory,
And, dying, mention it within their wills,
Bequeathing it as a rich legacy
Unto their issue.

FOURTH CITIZEN We'll hear the will: read it, Mark Antony.

ALL   The will, the will! we will hear Caesar's
             will.

ANTONY   Have patience, gentle friends, I must not
             read it;
             It is not meet you know how Caesar
             loved you.
             You are not wood, you are not stones,
             but men;
             And, being men, hearing the will of Caesar,
             It will inflame you, it will make you mad:
             'Tis good you know not that you are
             his heirs;

	For, if you should, O, what would come of it!
FOURTH CITIZEN	Read the will; we'll hear it, Antony;
	You shall read us the will, Caesar's will.
ANTONY	Will you be patient? will you stay awhile?
	I have o'ershot myself to tell you of it:
	I fear I wrong the honourable men
	Whose daggers have stabb'd Caesar; I do fear it.
FOURTH CITIZEN	They were traitors: honourable men!
ALL	The will! the testament!
SECOND CITIZEN	They were villains, murderers: the will! read the will.
ANTONY	You will compel me, then, to read the will?
	Then make a ring about the corpse of Caesar,
	And let me show you him that made the will.
	Shall I descend? and will you give me leave?
SEVERAL CITIZENS	Come down.
SECOND CITIZEN	Descend.
THIRD CITIZEN	You shall have leave.

ANTONY *comes down*

FOURTH CITIZEN	A ring; stand round.
FIRST CITIZEN	Stand from the hearse, stand from the body.
SECOND CITIZEN	Room for Antony, most noble Antony.
ANTONY	Nay, press not so upon me; stand far off.
SEVERAL CITIZENS	Stand back; room; bear back.
ANTONY	If you have tears, prepare to shed them now.

You all do know this mantle: I remember
The first time ever Caesar put it on;
'Twas on a summer's evening, in his tent,
That day he overcame the Nervii:
Look, in this place ran Cassius' dagger
through:
See what a rent the envious Casca made:
Through this the well-beloved Brutus
stabb'd;
And as he pluck'd his cursed steel away,
Mark how the blood of Caesar follow'd it,
As rushing out of doors, to be resolved
If Brutus so unkindly knock'd, or no;
For Brutus, as you know, was Caesar's
angel:
Judge, O you gods, how dearly Caesar
loved him!
This was the most unkindest cut of all;
For when the noble Caesar saw him stab,
Ingratitude, more strong than traitors'
arms,
Quite vanquish'd him: then burst his
mighty heart;
And, in his mantle muffling up his face,
Even at the base of Pompey's statua,
Which all the while ran blood, great Caesar
fell.
O, what a fall was there, my countrymen!
Then I, and you, and all of us fell down,

Whilst bloody treason flourish'd over us.
O, now you weep; and, I perceive, you feel
The dint of pity: these are gracious drops.
Kind souls, what, weep you when you but
behold
Our Caesar's vesture wounded? Look you
here,
Here is himself, marr'd, as you see, with
traitors.

FIRST CITIZEN   O piteous spectacle!

SECOND CITIZEN   O noble Caesar!

THIRD CITIZEN   O woeful day!

FOURTH CITIZEN   O traitors, villains!

FIRST CITIZEN   O most bloody sight!

SECOND CITIZEN   We will be revenged.

ALL   Revenge! About! Seek! Burn! Fire! Kill!
                 Slay!
                 Let not a traitor live!

ANTONY   Stay, countrymen.

FIRST CITIZEN   Peace there! hear the noble Antony.

SECOND CITIZEN   We'll hear him, we'll follow him, we'll die
                 with him.

ANTONY   Good friends, sweet friends, let me not stir
                 you up
                 To such a sudden flood of mutiny.
                 They that have done this deed are
                 honourable:
                 What private griefs they have, alas,
                 I know not,

That made them do it: they are wise and
honourable,
And will, no doubt, with reasons
answer you.
I come not, friends, to steal away your
hearts:
I am no orator, as Brutus is;
But, as you know me all, a plain
blunt man,
That love my friend; and that they know
full well
That gave me public leave to speak of him:
For I have neither wit, nor words,
 nor worth,
Action, nor utterance, nor the power of
speech,
To stir men's blood: I only speak right on;
I tell you that which you yourselves
do know;
Show you sweet Caesar's wounds, poor
poor dumb mouths,
And bid them speak for me: but were I
Brutus,
And Brutus Antony, there were an Antony
Would ruffle up your spirits and put a
tongue
In every wound of Caesar that should
move
The stones of Rome to rise and mutiny.

ALL	We'll mutiny.
FIRST CITIZEN	We'll burn the house of Brutus.
THIRD CITIZEN	Away, then! come, seek the conspirators.
ANTONY	Yet hear me, countrymen; yet hear me speak.
ALL	Peace, ho! Hear Antony. Most noble Antony!
ANTONY	Why, friends, you go to do you know not what:
	Wherein hath Caesar thus deserved your loves?
	Alas, you know not: I must tell you then:
	You have forgot the will I told you of.
ALL	Most true. The will! Let's stay and hear the will.
ANTONY	Here is the will, and under Caesar's seal.
	To every Roman citizen he gives,
	To every several man, seventy-five drachmas.
SECOND CITIZEN	Most noble Caesar! We'll revenge his death.
THIRD CITIZEN	O royal Caesar!
ANTONY	Hear me with patience.
ALL	Peace, ho!
ANTONY	Moreover, he hath left you all his walks,
	His private arbours and new-planted orchards,
	On this side Tiber; he hath left them you,
	And to your heirs for ever, common pleasures,

	To walk abroad, and recreate yourselves.
	Here was a Caesar! when comes such
	another?
FIRST CITIZEN	Never, never. Come, away, away!
	We'll burn his body in the holy place,
	And with the brands fire the traitors'
	houses.
	Take up the body.
SECOND CITIZEN	Go fetch fire.
THIRD CITIZEN	Pluck down benches.
FOURTH CITIZEN	Pluck down forms, windows, any thing.

Exeunt Citizens with the body

| ANTONY | Now let it work. Mischief, thou art afoot, |
| | Take thou what course thou wilt! |

10. The Power of Mercy

'O, it is excellent
To have a giant's strength; but it is tyrannous
To use it like a giant.'

From MEASURE FOR MEASURE

The Duke of Vienna has appointed Angelo his deputy. Angelo has sentenced Claudio to death for breaking a long-forgotten law. Claudio's sister Isabella and his friend Lucio visit Angelo to plead for mercy.

ACT II, SCENE II

ISABELLA   Must he needs die?

ANGELO   Maiden, no remedy.

ISABELLA   Yes; I do think that you might pardon him,
And neither heaven nor man grieve at the
mercy.

ANGELO   I will not do't.

ISABELLA   But can you, if you would?

ANGELO   Look, what I will not, that I cannot do.

ISABELLA   But might you do't, and do the world no wrong,
If so your heart were touch'd with that remorse
As mine is to him?

ANGELO   He's sentenced; 'tis too late.

LUCIO   [*Aside to* ISABELLA]
You are too cold.

ISABELLA   Too late? Why, no; I, that do speak a word,
May call it back again. Well, believe this,
No ceremony that to great ones 'longs,
Not the king's crown, nor the deputed sword,
The marshal's truncheon, nor the judge's robe,
Become them with one half so good a grace
As mercy does.
If he had been as you and you as he,
You would have slipt like him; but he, like you,
Would not have been so stern.

ANGELO   Pray you, be gone.

ISABELLA   I would to heaven I had your potency,

And you were Isabel! Should it then be thus?
No; I would tell what 'twere to be a judge,
And what a prisoner.

LUCIO   [*Aside to* ISABELLA]
             Ay, touch him; there's the vein.

ANGELO   Your brother is a forfeit of the law,
             And you but waste your words.

ISABELLA   Alas, alas!
             Why, all the souls that were were forfeit once;
             And He that might the vantage best have took
             Found out the remedy. How would you be,
             If He, which is the top of judgment, should
             But judge you as you are? O, think on that;
             And mercy then will breathe within your lips,
             Like man new made.

ANGELO   Be you content, fair maid;
             It is the law, not I, condemn your brother:
             Were he my kinsman, brother, or my son,
             It should be thus with him: he must die
             tomorrow.

ISABELLA   To-morrow! O, that's sudden! Spare him,
             spare him!
             He's not prepared for death. Even for our kitchens
             We kill the fowl of season: shall we serve heaven
             With less respect than we do minister
             To our gross selves? Good, good my lord,
             bethink you;
             Who is it that hath died for this offence?
             There's many have committed it.

LUCIO	[*Aside to* ISABELLA]
	Ay, well said.
ANGELO	The law hath not been dead, though it hath slept:
	Those many had not dared to do that evil,
	If the first that did the edict infringe
	Had answer'd for his deed: now 'tis awake,
	Takes note of what is done; and, like a prophet,
	Looks in a glass that shows what future evils,
	Either new, or by remissness new-conceived,
	And so in progress to be hatch'd and born,
	Are now to have no successive degrees,
	But, ere they live, to end.
ISABELLA	Yet show some pity.
ANGELO	I show it most of all when I show justice;
	For then I pity those I do not know,
	Which a dismiss'd offence would after gall;
	And do him right that, answering one foul
	wrong,
	Lives not to act another. Be satisfied;
	Your brother dies to-morrow; be content.
ISABELLA	So you must be the first that gives this sentence,
	And he, that suffers. O, it is excellent
	To have a giant's strength; but it is tyrannous
	To use it like a giant.
LUCIO	[*Aside to* ISABELLA]
	That's well said.
ISABELLA	Could great men thunder
	As Jove himself does, Jove would ne'er be quiet,
	For every pelting, petty officer

Would use his heaven for thunder;
Nothing but thunder! Merciful Heaven,
Thou rather with thy sharp and sulphurous bolt
Split'st the unwedgeable and gnarled oak
Than the soft myrtle: but man, proud man,
Drest in a little brief authority,
Most ignorant of what he's most assured,
His glassy essence, like an angry ape,
Plays such fantastic tricks before high heaven
As make the angels weep; who, with our spleens,
Would all themselves laugh mortal.

LUCIO   [*Aside to* ISABELLA]
O, to him, to him, wench! He will relent;
He's coming; I perceive 't.

PROVOST   [*Aside*]
Pray heaven she win him!

ISABELLA   We cannot weigh our brother with ourself:
Great men may jest with saints; 'tis wit in them,
But in the less foul profanation.

LUCIO   Thou'rt i' the right, girl; more o, that.

ISABELLA   That in the captain's but a choleric word,
Which in the soldier is flat blasphemy.

LUCIO   [*Aside to* ISABELLA]
Art avised o' that? More on 't.

ANGELO   Why do you put these sayings upon me?

ISABELLA   Because authority, though it err like others,
Hath yet a kind of medicine in itself,
That skins the vice o' the top. Go to your
bosom;

Knock there, and ask your heart what it
doth know
That's like my brother's fault: if it confess
A natural guiltiness such as is his,
Let it not sound a thought upon your tongue
Against my brother's life.

ANGELO   [*Aside*]
She speaks, and 'tis
Such sense, that my sense breeds with it. Fare
you well.

11. The Burden of Power

> 'What infinite heart's-ease
> Must kings neglect, that private men enjoy!'

From HENRY V

In the early hours of the morning, King Henry walks in disguise among his soldiers who will soon fight a battle against the French army. The English forces are outnumbered and face almost certain defeat. Bates, Court and Williams are rank and file soldiers, who most likely have never seen their king face to face before.

ACT IV, SCENE I

COURT	Brother John Bates, is not that the morning which breaks yonder?
BATES	I think it be: but we have no great cause to desire the approach of day.
WILLIAMS	We see yonder the beginning of the day, but I think we shall never see the end of it. Who goes there?
KING HENRY V	A friend.
WILLIAMS	Under what captain serve you?
KING HENRY V	Under Sir Thomas Erpingham.
WILLIAMS	A good old commander and a most kind gentleman: I pray you, what thinks he of our estate?
KING HENRY V	Even as men wrecked upon a sand, that look to be washed off the next tide.
BATES	He hath not told his thought to the king?
KING HENRY V	No; nor it is not meet he should. For, though I speak it to you, I think the king is but a man, as I am: the violet smells to him as it doth to me; the element shows to him as it doth to me; all his senses have but human conditions: his ceremonies laid by, in his nakedness he appears but a man; and though his affections are higher mounted than ours, yet, when they stoop, they stoop with the

like wing. Therefore when he sees reason of
fears, as we do, his fears, out of doubt, be
of the same relish as ours are: yet, in reason,
no man should possess him with any
appearance of fear, lest he, by showing it,
should dishearten his army.

BATES He may show what outward courage he will;
but I believe, as cold a night as 'tis, he could
wish himself in Thames up to the neck; and
so I would he were, and I by him, at all
adventures, so we were quit here.

KING HENRY V By my troth, I will speak my conscience of
the king: I think he would not wish himself
any where but where he is.

BATES Then I would he were here alone; so should
he be sure to be ransomed, and a many poor
men's lives saved.

KING HENRY V I dare say you love him not so ill, to wish
him here alone, howsoever you speak this to
feel other men's minds: methinks I could not
die any where so contented as in the king's
company; his cause being just and his
quarrel honourable.

WILLIAMS That's more than we know.

BATES Ay, or more than we should seek after; for we
know enough if we know we are the king's
subjects: if his cause be wrong, our
obedience to the king wipes the crime of it
out of us.

WILLIAMS   But if the cause be not good, the king himself hath a heavy reckoning to make, when all those legs and arms and heads, chopped off in battle, shall join together at the latter day and cry all, 'We died at such a place'; some swearing, some crying for a surgeon, some upon their wives left poor behind them, some upon the debts they owe, some upon their children rawly left. I am afeard there are few die well that die in a battle; for how can they charitably dispose of any thing, when blood is their argument? Now, if these men do not die well, it will be a black matter for the king that led them to it; whom to disobey were against all proportion of subjection.

KING HENRY V   So, if a son that is by his father sent about merchandise do sinfully miscarry upon the sea, the imputation of his wickedness, by your rule, should be imposed upon his father that sent him: or if a servant, under his master's command transporting a sum of money, be assailed by robbers and die in many irreconciled iniquities, you may call the business of the master the author of the servant's damnation: but this is not so: the king is not bound to answer the particular endings of his soldiers, the father of his son, nor the master of his servant; for they purpose not their death, when they purpose their services. Besides, there is no king, be his cause never so spotless, if it come to the arbitrement of swords, can try it out with all unspotted soldiers: some peradventure have on them the guilt of premeditated and contrived murder; some, of beguiling virgins with the broken seals of perjury; some, making the wars their bulwark, that have before gored the gentle bosom of peace with pillage and robbery. Now, if these men have defeated the law and outrun native punishment, though they can outstrip men, they have no wings to fly from God: war is his beadle, war is his vengeance; so that here men are punished for before-breach of the king's laws in now the king's quarrel: where they feared the death, they have borne life away; and where they would be safe, they perish: then if they die unprovided, no more is the king guilty of their damnation than he was before guilty of those impieties for the which they are now visited. Every subject's duty is the king's; but every subject's soul is his own. Therefore should every soldier in the wars do as every sick man in his bed, wash every mote out of his conscience: and dying so, death is to him advantage; or not dying, the time was blessedly lost wherein

such preparation was gained: and in him
that escapes, it were not sin to think that,
making God so free an offer, He let him
outlive that day to see His greatness and to
teach others how they should prepare.

WILLIAMS 'Tis certain, every man that dies ill, the ill
upon his own head, the king is not to
answer it.

BATES But I do not desire he should answer for me;
and yet I determine to fight lustily for him.

KING HENRY V I myself heard the king say he would not be
ransomed.

WILLIAMS Ay, he said so, to make us fight cheerfully:
but when our throats are cut, he may be
ransomed, and we ne'er the wiser.

KING HENRY V If I live to see it, I will never trust his word
after.

WILLIAMS You pay him then. That's a perilous shot out
of an elder-gun, that a poor and private
displeasure can do against a monarch! You
may as well go about to turn the sun to ice
with fanning in his face with a peacock's
feather. You'll never trust his word after!
Come, 'tis a foolish saying.

KING HENRY V Your reproof is something too round: I
should be angry with you, if the time were
convenient.

WILLIAMS Let it be a quarrel between us, if you live.

KING HENRY V I embrace it.

WILLIAMS	How shall I know thee again?
KING HENRY V	Give me any gage of thine, and I will wear it in my bonnet: then, if ever thou darest acknowledge it, I will make it my quarrel.
WILLIAMS	Here's my glove: give me another of thine.
KING HENRY V	There.
WILLIAMS	This will I also wear in my cap: if ever thou come to me and say, after to-morrow, 'This is my glove', by this hand, I will take thee a box on the ear.
KING HENRY V	If ever I live to see it, I will challenge it.
WILLIAMS	Thou darest as well be hanged.
KING HENRY V	Well, I will do it, though I take thee in the king's company.
WILLIAMS	Keep thy word: fare thee well.
BATES	Be friends, you English fools, be friends: we have French quarrels enow, if you could tell how to reckon.
KING HENRY V	Indeed, the French may lay twenty French crowns to one, they will beat us; for they bear them on their shoulders: but it is no English treason to cut French crowns, and to-morrow the king himself will be a clipper.

Exeunt soldiers

Upon the king! Let us our lives, our souls,
Our debts, our careful wives,
Our children and our sins lay on the king!

We must bear all. O hard condition,
Twin-born with greatness, subject to
the breath
Of every fool, whose sense no more can feel
But his own wringing! What infinite
heart's-ease
Must kings neglect, that private men enjoy!
And what have kings, that privates have
not too,
Save ceremony, save general ceremony?
And what art thou, thou idle ceremony?
What kind of god art thou, that suffer'st more
Of mortal griefs than do thy worshippers?
What are thy rents? What are thy comings in?
O ceremony, show me but thy worth!
What is thy soul of adoration?
Art thou aught else but place, degree
and form,
Creating awe and fear in other men?
Wherein thou art less happy being fear'd
Than they in fearing.
What drink'st thou oft, instead of
homage sweet,
But poison'd flattery? O, be sick, great
greatness,
And bid thy ceremony give thee cure!
Think'st thou the fiery fever will go out
With titles blown from adulation?
Will it give place to flexure and low bending?

Canst thou, when thou command'st the
beggar's knee,
Command the health of it? No, thou proud
dream,
That play'st so subtly with a king's repose;
I am a king that find thee, and I know
'Tis not the balm, the sceptre and the ball,
The sword, the mace, the crown imperial,
The intertissued robe of gold and pearl,
The farced title running 'fore the king,
The throne he sits on, nor the tide of pomp
That beats upon the high shore of this world,
No, not all these, thrice-gorgeous ceremony,
Not all these, laid in bed majestical,
Can sleep so soundly as the wretched slave,
Who with a body fill'd and vacant mind
Gets him to rest, cramm'd with distressful
bread;
Never sees horrid night, the child of hell,
But, like a lackey, from the rise to set
Sweats in the eye of Phoebus and all night
Sleeps in Elysium; next day after dawn,
Doth rise and help Hyperion to his horse,
And follows so the ever-running year,
With profitable labour, to his grave:
And, but for ceremony, such a wretch,
Winding up days with toil and nights
with sleep,
Had the fore-hand and vantage of a king.

The slave, a member of the country's peace,
Enjoys it; but in gross brain little wots
What watch the king keeps to maintain
the peace,
Whose hours the peasant best advantages.

12. The Fall from Power

'Within the hollow crown
That rounds the mortal temples of a king
Keeps Death his court.'

From RICHARD II

John of Gaunt, Duke of Lancaster, has died and King Richard has unlawfully seized his lands and property, provoking a rebellion among his nobles and subjects who rally round Gaunt's exiled son, Henry Bolingbroke.

ACT III, SCENE II

The coast of Wales. A castle in view. Drums;
flourish and colours. Enter KING RICHARD II, *the* BISHOP OF
CARLISLE, DUKE OF AUMERLE, *and Soldiers*

KING RICHARD II	Barkloughly Castle call they this at hand?
DUKE OF AUMERLE	Yea, my lord. How brooks your grace the air, After your late tossing on the breaking seas?
KING RICHARD II	Needs must I like it well: I weep for joy To stand upon my kingdom once again. Dear earth, I do salute thee with my hand, Though rebels wound thee with their horses' hoofs: As a long-parted mother with her child Plays fondly with her tears and smiles in meeting, So, weeping, smiling, greet I thee, my earth, And do thee favours with my royal hands. Feed not thy sovereign's foe, my gentle earth, Nor with thy sweets comfort his ravenous sense;

But let thy spiders, that suck up
thy venom,
And heavy-gaited toads lie in their way,
Doing annoyance to the treacherous feet
Which with usurping steps do
trample thee:
Yield stinging nettles to mine enemies;
And when they from thy bosom
pluck a flower,
Guard it, I pray thee, with a lurking adder
Whose double tongue may with a
mortal touch
Throw death upon thy sovereign's
enemies.
Mock not my senseless conjuration,
lords:
This earth shall have a feeling and these
stones
Prove armed soldiers, ere her native king
Shall falter under foul rebellion's arms.

BISHOP OF CARLISLE Fear not, my lord: that Power that made
you king
Hath power to keep you king in spite
of all.
The means that heaven yields must be
embraced,
And not neglected; else, if heaven would,
And we will not, heaven's offer we
refuse,

The proffer'd means of succor and
redress.

DUKE OF AUMERLE   He means, my lord, that we are too
remiss;
Whilst Bolingbroke, through our
security,
Grows strong and great in substance
and in power.

KING RICHARD II   Discomfortable cousin! know'st thou not
That when the searching eye of heaven
is hid,
Behind the globe, that lights the lower
world,
Then thieves and robbers range abroad
unseen
In murders and in outrage, boldly here;
But when from under this terrestrial ball
He fires the proud tops of the
eastern pines
And darts his light through every guilty
hole,
Then murders, treasons and detested
sins,
The cloak of night being pluck'd from
off their backs,
Stand bare and naked, trembling at
themselves?
So when this thief, this traitor,
Bolingbroke,

Who all this while hath revell'd in
the night
Whilst we were wandering with the
antipodes,
Shall see us rising in our throne,
the east,
His treasons will sit blushing in his face,
Not able to endure the sight of day,
But self-affrighted tremble at his sin.
Not all the water in the rough rude sea
Can wash the balm off from an
anointed king;
The breath of worldly men cannot
depose
The deputy elected by the Lord:
For every man that Bolingbroke hath
press'd
To lift shrewd steel against our golden
crown,
God for his Richard hath in heavenly pay
A glorious angel: then, if angels fight,
Weak men must fall, for heaven still
guards the right.

Enter EARL OF SALISBURY

Welcome, my lord how far off lies your
power?

EARL OF SALISBURY Nor near nor farther off, my gracious
lord,

Than this weak arm: discomfort guides
my tongue
And bids me speak of nothing but
despair.
One day too late, I fear me, noble lord,
Hath clouded all thy happy days on
earth:
O, call back yesterday, bid time return,
And thou shalt have twelve thousand
fighting men!
To-day, to-day, unhappy day, too late,
O'erthrows thy joys, friends, fortune
and thy state:
For all the Welshmen, hearing thou
wert dead,
Are gone to Bolingbroke, dispersed and
fled.

DUKE OF AUMERLE   Comfort, my liege; why looks your grace
so pale?

KING RICHARD II   But now the blood of twenty
thousand men
Did triumph in my face, and they
are fled;
And, till so much blood thither
come again,
Have I not reason to look pale and dead?
All souls that will be safe fly from
my side,
For time hath set a blot upon my pride.

DUKE OF AUMERLE	Comfort, my liege; remember who you are.
KING RICHARD II	I had forgot myself; am I not king?
	Awake, thou coward majesty! thou sleepest.
	Is not the king's name twenty thousand names?
	Arm, arm, my name! a puny subject strikes
	At thy great glory. Look not to the ground,
	Ye favourites of a king: are we not high?
	High be our thoughts: I know my uncle York
	Hath power enough to serve our turn.
	But who comes here?

Enter SIR STEPHEN SCROOP

SIR STEPHEN SCROOP	More health and happiness betide my liege
	Than can my care-tuned tongue deliver him!
KING RICHARD II	Mine ear is open and my heart prepared;
	The worst is worldly loss thou canst unfold.
	Say, is my kingdom lost? why, 'twas my care
	And what loss is it to be rid of care?
	Strives Bolingbroke to be as great as we?

Greater he shall not be; if he serve God,
We'll serve Him too and be his fellow so:
Revolt our subjects? that we cannot
mend;
They break their faith to God as well
as us:
Cry woe, destruction, ruin and decay:
The worst is death, and death will have
his day.

SIR STEPHEN SCROOP Glad am I that your highness is so arm'd
To bear the tidings of calamity.
Like an unseasonable stormy day,
Which makes the silver rivers drown
their shores,
As if the world were all dissolved
to tears,
So high above his limits swells the rage
Of Bolingbroke, covering your fearful
land
With hard bright steel and hearts
harder than steel.
White-beards have arm'd their thin and
hairless scalps
Against thy majesty; boys, with
women's voices,
Strive to speak big and clap their female
joints
In stiff unwieldy arms against thy
crown:

The very beadsmen learn to bend
their bows
Of double-fatal yew against thy state;
Yea, distaff-women manage rusty bills
Against thy seat: both young and
old rebel,
And all goes worse than I have power
to tell.

KING RICHARD II   Too well, too well thou tell'st a
tale so ill.
Where is the Earl of Wiltshire? where is
Bagot?
What is become of Bushy? where is
Green?
That they have let the dangerous enemy
Measure our confines with such
peaceful steps?
If we prevail, their heads shall pay for it:
I warrant they have made peace with
Bolingbroke.

SIR STEPHEN SCROOP   Peace have they made with him indeed,
my lord.

KING RICHARD II   O villains, vipers, damn'd without
redemption!
Dogs, easily won to fawn on any man!
Snakes, in my heart-blood warm'd, that
sting my heart!
Three Judases, each one thrice worse
than Judas!

	Would they make peace? terrible hell make war
	Upon their spotted souls for this offence!
SIR STEPHEN SCROOP	Sweet love, I see, changing his property,
	Turns to the sourest and most deadly hate:
	Again uncurse their souls; their peace is made
	With heads, and not with hands; those whom you curse
	Have felt the worst of death's destroying wound
	And lie full low, graved in the hollow ground.
DUKE OF AUMERLE	Is Bushy, Green, and the Earl of Wiltshire dead?
SIR STEPHEN SCROOP	Ay, all of them at Bristol lost their heads.
DUKE OF AUMERLE	Where is the duke my father with his power?
KING RICHARD II	No matter where; of comfort no man speak:
	Let's talk of graves, of worms, and epitaphs;
	Make dust our paper and with rainy eyes
	Write sorrow on the bosom of the earth,
	Let's choose executors and talk of wills:
	And yet not so, for what can we bequeath

Save our deposed bodies to the ground?
Our lands, our lives and all are
Bolingbroke's,
And nothing can we call our own
but death
And that small model of the barren earth
Which serves as paste and cover to
our bones.
For God's sake, let us sit upon the ground
And tell sad stories of the death of kings;
How some have been deposed; some
slain in war,
Some haunted by the ghosts they
have deposed;
Some poison'd by their wives: some
sleeping kill'd;
All murder'd: for within the hollow
crown
That rounds the mortal temples of a king
Keeps Death his court and there the
antic sits,
Scoffing his state and grinning at his
pomp,
Allowing him a breath, a little scene,
To monarchize, be fear'd and kill with
looks,
Infusing him with self and vain conceit,
As if this flesh which walls about
our life,

Were brass impregnable, and
humour'd thus
Comes at the last and with a little pin
Bores through his castle wall, and
farewell king!
Cover your heads and mock not flesh
and blood
With solemn reverence: throw away
respect,
Tradition, form and ceremonious duty,
For you have but mistook me all
this while:
I live with bread like you, feel want,
Taste grief, need friends: subjected
thus,
How can you say to me, I am a king?

BISHOP OF CARLISLE My lord, wise men ne'er sit and wail
their woes,
But presently prevent the ways to wail.
To fear the foe, since fear oppresseth
strength,
Gives in your weakness strength unto
your foe,
And so your follies fight against
yourself.
Fear and be slain; no worse can come to
fight:
And fight and die is death destroying
death,

Where fearing dying pays death servile
breath.

DUKE OF AUMERLE My father hath a power; inquire of him
And learn to make a body of a limb.

KING RICHARD II Thou chidest me well: proud
Bolingbroke, I come
To change blows with thee for our day
of doom.
This ague fit of fear is over-blown;
An easy task it is to win our own.
Say, Scroop, where lies our uncle with
his power?
Speak sweetly, man, although thy looks
be sour.

SIR STEPHEN SCROOP Men judge by the complexion of the sky
The state and inclination of the day:
So may you by my dull and heavy eye,
My tongue hath but a heavier tale to say.
I play the torturer, by small and small
To lengthen out the worst that must be
spoken:
Your uncle York is join'd with
Bolingbroke,
And all your northern castles yielded up,
And all your southern gentlemen in arms
Upon his party.

KING RICHARD II Thou hast said enough.
Beshrew thee, cousin, which didst lead
me forth

To DUKE OF AUMERLE

Of that sweet way I was in to despair!
What say you now? what comfort have
we now?
By heaven, I'll hate him everlastingly
That bids me be of comfort any more.
Go to Flint castle: there I'll pine away;
A king, woe's slave, shall kingly woe obey.
That power I have, discharge; and
let them go
To ear the land that hath some
hope to grow,
For I have none: let no man speak again
To alter this, for counsel is but vain.

DUKE OF AUMERLE   My liege, one word.

KING RICHARD II   He does me double wrong
That wounds me with the flatteries of
his tongue.
Discharge my followers: let them hence
away,
From Richard's night to Bolingbroke's
fair day.

13. The Illusion of Power

> 'Now my charms are all o'erthrown,
> And what strength I have's mine own'

Prospero was formerly the Duke of Naples, but was deposed by his brother Antonio, with help from Alonso, King of Naples, and the King's brother Sebastian. On a remote island, Prospero has become a powerful sorcerer and has in his command a sprite named Ariel. Miranda is Prospero's daughter. Caliban is a witch's son, and the only other inhabitant of the island. With Ariel's help, Prospero has brought Antonio, Sebastian, Alonso and his son Ferdinand, and their followers, the drunken Stephano and Trinculo, to the island for a final reckoning.

ACT V, SCENE I

Enter PROSPERO *in his magic robes, and* ARIEL

PROSPERO   Now does my project gather to a head:
            My charms crack not; my spirits obey; and time
            Goes upright with his carriage. How's the day?

ARIEL   On the sixth hour; at which time, my lord,
            You said our work should cease.

PROSPERO   I did say so,
            When first I raised the tempest. Say, my spirit,
            How fares the king and's followers?

ARIEL   Confined together
            In the same fashion as you gave in charge,
            Just as you left them; all prisoners, sir,
            In the line-grove which weather-fends your cell;
            They cannot budge till your release. The king,
            His brother, and yours, abide all three distracted
            And the remainder mourning over them,
            Brimful of sorrow and dismay; but chiefly
            Him that you term'd, sir, 'The good old lord
            Gonzalo';
            His tears run down his beard, like winter's drops
            From eaves of reeds. Your charm so strongly
            works 'em
            That if you now beheld them, your affections
            Would become tender.

PROSPERO   Dost thou think so, spirit?

ARIEL   Mine would, sir, were I human.

PROSPERO   And mine shall.

            Hast thou, which art but air, a touch, a feeling
            Of their afflictions, and shall not myself,
            One of their kind, that relish all as sharply,
            Passion as they, be kindlier moved than thou art?
            Though with their high wrongs I am struck to
            the quick,
            Yet with my nobler reason 'gainst my fury
            Do I take part: the rarer action is
            In virtue than in vengeance: they being penitent,
            The sole drift of my purpose doth extend
            Not a frown further. Go release them, Ariel:
            My charms I'll break, their senses I'll restore,
            And they shall be themselves.

ARIEL   I'll fetch them, sir.

                        Exit

PROSPERO   Ye elves of hills, brooks, standing lakes and
            groves,
            And ye that on the sands with printless foot
            Do chase the ebbing Neptune and do fly him
            When he comes back; you demi-puppets that
            By moonshine do the green sour ringlets make,
            Whereof the ewe not bites, and you whose
            pastime
            Is to make midnight mushrooms, that rejoice
            To hear the solemn curfew; by whose aid,
            Weak masters though ye be, I have bedimm'd

The noontide sun, call'd forth the mutinous
winds,
And 'twixt the green sea and the azured vault
Set roaring war: to the dread rattling thunder
Have I given fire and rifted Jove's stout oak
With his own bolt; the strong-based
promontory
Have I made shake and by the spurs pluck'd up
The pine and cedar: graves at my command
Have waked their sleepers, oped, and let 'em forth
By my so potent art. But this rough magic
I here abjure, and, when I have required
Some heavenly music, which even now I do,
To work mine end upon their senses that
This airy charm is for, I'll break my staff,
Bury it certain fathoms in the earth,
And deeper than did ever plummet sound
I'll drown my book.

Solemn music

Re-enter ARIEL *before: then* ALONSO, *with a frantic gesture,
attended by* GONZALO; SEBASTIAN *and* ANTONIO *in like
manner, attended by* ADRIAN *and* FRANCISCO: *they all
enter the circle which* PROSPERO *had made,
and there stand charmed; which*
PROSPERO *observing, speaks:*

A solemn air and the best comforter
To an unsettled fancy cure thy brains,

Now useless, boil'd within thy skull! There stand,
For you are spell-stopp'd.
Holy Gonzalo, honourable man,
Mine eyes, even sociable to the show of thine,
Fall fellowly drops. The charm dissolves apace,
And as the morning steals upon the night,
Melting the darkness, so their rising senses
Begin to chase the ignorant fumes that mantle
Their clearer reason. O good Gonzalo,
My true preserver, and a loyal sir
To him you follow'st! I will pay thy graces
Home both in word and deed. Most cruelly
Didst thou, Alonso, use me and my daughter:
Thy brother was a furtherer in the act.
Thou art pinch'd for't now, Sebastian. Flesh and
blood,
You, brother mine, that entertain'd ambition,
Expell'd remorse and nature; who, with
Sebastian,
Whose inward pinches therefore are most strong,
Would here have kill'd your king; I do forgive
thee,
Unnatural though thou art. Their
understanding
Begins to swell, and the approaching tide
Will shortly fill the reasonable shore
That now lies foul and muddy. Not one of them
That yet looks on me, or would know me. Ariel,
Fetch me the hat and rapier in my cell:

I will discase me, and myself present
As I was sometime Milan: quickly, spirit;
Thou shalt ere long be free.

ARIEL   *sings and helps to attire him*
Where the bee sucks, there suck I:
In a cowslip's bell I lie;
There I couch when owls do cry.
On the bat's back I do fly
After summer merrily.
Merrily, merrily shall I live now
Under the blossom that hangs on the bough.

PROSPERO   Why, that's my dainty Ariel! I shall miss thee:
But yet thou shalt have freedom: so, so, so.
To the king's ship, invisible as thou art:
There shalt thou find the mariners asleep
Under the hatches; the master and the
boatswain
Being awake, enforce them to this place,
And presently, I prithee.

ARIEL   I drink the air before me, and return
Or ere your pulse twice beat.

Exit

GONZALO   All torment, trouble, wonder and amazement
Inhabits here: some heavenly power guide us
Out of this fearful country!

PROSPERO   Behold, sir king,
The wronged Duke of Milan, Prospero:
For more assurance that a living prince

	Does now speak to thee, I embrace thy body;
	And to thee and thy company I bid
	A hearty welcome.
ALONSO	Whether thou be'st he or no,
	Or some enchanted trifle to abuse me,
	As late I have been, I not know: thy pulse
	Beats as of flesh and blood; and, since I saw thee,
	The affliction of my mind amends, with which,
	I fear, a madness held me: this must crave,
	An if this be at all, a most strange story.
	Thy dukedom I resign and do entreat
	Thou pardon me my wrongs. But how should Prospero
	Be living and be here?
PROSPERO	First, noble friend,
	Let me embrace thine age, whose honour cannot
	Be measured or confined.
GONZALO	Whether this be
	Or be not, I'll not swear.
PROSPERO	You do yet taste
	Some subtilties o' the isle, that will not let you
	Believe things certain. Welcome, my friends all!

Aside to SEBASTIAN *and* ANTONIO

But you, my brace of lords, were I so minded,
I here could pluck his highness' frown upon you
And justify you traitors: at this time
I will tell no tales.

SEBASTIAN [*Aside*]
                 The devil speaks in him.
PROSPERO   No.
                 For you, most wicked sir, whom to call brother
                 Would even infect my mouth, I do forgive
                 Thy rankest fault; all of them; and require
                 My dukedom of thee, which perforce, I know,
                 Thou must restore.
ALONSO   If thou be'st Prospero,
                 Give us particulars of thy preservation;
                 How thou hast met us here, who three hours
                 since
                 Were wreck'd upon this shore; where I have lost—
                 How sharp the point of this remembrance is!—
                 My dear son Ferdinand.
PROSPERO   I am woe for't, sir.
ALONSO   Irreparable is the loss, and patience
                 Says it is past her cure.
PROSPERO   I rather think
                 You have not sought her help, of whose soft
                 grace
                 For the like loss I have her sovereign aid
                 And rest myself content.
ALONSO   You the like loss!
PROSPERO   As great to me as late; and, supportable
                 To make the dear loss, have I means much
                 weaker
                 Than you may call to comfort you, for I
                 Have lost my daughter.

ALONSO   A daughter?
O heavens, that they were living both in Naples,
The king and queen there! that they were,
I wish
Myself were mudded in that oozy bed
Where my son lies. When did you lose your
daughter?

PROSPERO   In this last tempest. I perceive these lords
At this encounter do so much admire
That they devour their reason and scarce think
Their eyes do offices of truth, their words
Are natural breath: but, howsoe'er you have
Been justled from your senses, know for
certain
That I am Prospero and that very duke
Which was thrust forth of Milan, who most
strangely
Upon this shore, where you were wreck'd, was
landed,
To be the lord on't. No more yet of this;
For 'tis a chronicle of day by day,
Not a relation for a breakfast nor
Befitting this first meeting. Welcome, sir;
This cell's my court: here have I few attendants
And subjects none abroad: pray you, look in.
My dukedom since you have given me again,
I will requite you with as good a thing;
At least bring forth a wonder, to content ye
As much as me my dukedom.

Here PROSPERO *shows*
FERDINAND *and* MIRANDA *playing at chess*

MIRANDA   Sweet lord, you play me false.

FERDINAND   No, my dear'st love,
             I would not for the world.

MIRANDA   Yes, for a score of kingdoms you should wrangle,
             And I would call it fair play.

ALONSO   If this prove
             A vision of the island, one dear son
             Shall I twice lose.

SEBASTIAN   A most high miracle!

FERDINAND   Though the seas threaten, they are merciful;
             I have cursed them without cause.

Kneels

ALONSO   Now all the blessings
             Of a glad father compass thee about!
             Arise, and say how thou camest here.

MIRANDA   O, wonder!
             How many goodly creatures are there here!
             How beauteous mankind is! O brave new world,
             That has such people in't!

PROSPERO   'Tis new to thee.

ALONSO   What is this maid with whom thou wast
             at play?
             Your eld'st acquaintance cannot be three hours:
             Is she the goddess that hath sever'd us,
             And brought us thus together?

FERDINAND   Sir, she is mortal;
But by immortal Providence she's mine:
I chose her when I could not ask
my father
For his advice, nor thought I had one. She
Is daughter to this famous Duke of Milan,
Of whom so often I have heard renown,
But never saw before; of whom I have
Received a second life; and second father
This lady makes him to me.

ALONSO   I am hers:
But, O, how oddly will it sound that I
Must ask my child forgiveness!

PROSPERO   There, sir, stop:
Let us not burthen our remembrance with
A heaviness that's gone.

GONZALO   I have inly wept,
Or should have spoke ere this. Look down,
you gods,
And on this couple drop a blessed crown!
For it is you that have chalk'd forth the way
Which brought us hither.

ALONSO   I say, Amen, Gonzalo!

GONZALO   Was Milan thrust from Milan, that his issue
Should become kings of Naples? O, rejoice
Beyond a common joy, and set it down
With gold on lasting pillars: In one voyage
Did Claribel her husband find at Tunis,
And Ferdinand, her brother, found a wife

Where he himself was lost, Prospero his
dukedom
In a poor isle and all of us ourselves
When no man was his own.

ALONSO   [*To* FERDINAND *and* MIRANDA]
Give me your hands:
Let grief and sorrow still embrace his heart
That doth not wish you joy!

GONZALO   Be it so! Amen!

Re-enter ARIEL, *with the Master and*
Boatswain amazedly following

O, look, sir, look, sir! here is more of us:
I prophesied, if a gallows were on land,
This fellow could not drown. Now, blasphemy,
That swear'st grace o'erboard, not an oath on
shore?
Hast thou no mouth by land? What is the news?

BOATSWAIN The best news is, that we have safely found
Our king and company; the next, our ship—
Which, but three glasses since, we gave out split—
Is tight and yare and bravely rigg'd as when
We first put out to sea.

ARIEL   [*Aside to* PROSPERO]
Sir, all this service
Have I done since I went.

PROSPERO [*Aside to* ARIEL]
My tricksy spirit!

ALONSO   These are not natural events; they strengthen

From strange to stranger. Say, how came you
hither?

BOATSWAIN If I did think, sir, I were well awake,
I'ld strive to tell you. We were dead of sleep,
And—how we know not—all clapp'd under
hatches;
Where but even now with strange and several
noises
Of roaring, shrieking, howling, jingling chains,
And more diversity of sounds, all horrible,
We were awaked; straightway, at liberty;
Where we, in all her trim, freshly beheld
Our royal, good and gallant ship, our master
Capering to eye her: on a trice, so please you,
Even in a dream, were we divided from them
And were brought moping hither.

ARIEL [*Aside to* PROSPERO]
Was't well done?

PROSPERO [*Aside to* ARIEL]
Bravely, my diligence. Thou shalt be free.

ALONSO This is as strange a maze as e'er men trod
And there is in this business more than nature
Was ever conduct of: some oracle
Must rectify our knowledge.

PROSPERO Sir, my liege,
Do not infest your mind with beating on
The strangeness of this business; at pick'd
leisure,
Which shall be shortly, single I'll resolve you,

Which to you shall seem probable, of every
These happen'd accidents; till when, be cheerful
And think of each thing well.
[*Aside to* ARIEL]
Come hither, spirit:
Set Caliban and his companions free;
Untie the spell.

Exit ARIEL

How fares my gracious sir?
There are yet missing of your company
Some few odd lads that you remember not.

Re-enter ARIEL, *driving in* CALIBAN, STEPHANO *and*
TRINCULO, *in their stolen apparel*

STEPHANO   Every man shift for all the rest, and
let no man take care for himself; for all is
but fortune. Coragio, bully-monster, coragio!

TRINCULO   If these be true spies which I wear in my head,
here's a goodly sight.

CALIBAN   O Setebos, these be brave spirits indeed!
How fine my master is! I am afraid
He will chastise me.

SEBASTIAN   Ha, ha!
What things are these, my lord Antonio?
Will money buy 'em?

ANTONIO   Very like; one of them
Is a plain fish, and, no doubt, marketable.

PROSPERO   Mark but the badges of these men, my lords,

Then say if they be true. This mis-shapen knave,
His mother was a witch, and one so strong
That could control the moon, make flows and
ebbs,
And deal in her command, without her power.
These three have robb'd me; and this demi-devil—
For he's a bastard one—had plotted with them
To take my life. Two of these fellows you
Must know and own; this thing of darkness I
Acknowledge mine.

CALIBAN   I shall be pinch'd to death.

ALONSO   Is not this Stephano, my drunken butler?

SEBASTIAN   He is drunk now: where had he wine?

ALONSO   And Trinculo is reeling ripe: where should they
             Find this grand liquor that hath gilded 'em?
             How camest thou in this pickle?

TRINCULO   I have been in such a pickle since I
             saw you last that, I fear me, will never out of
             my bones: I shall not fear fly-blowing.

SEBASTIAN   Why, how now, Stephano!

STEPHANO   O, touch me not; I am not Stephano, but a cramp.

PROSPERO   You'ld be king o' the isle, sirrah?

STEPHANO   I should have been a sore one then.

ALONSO   This is a strange thing as e'er I look'd on.

Pointing to Caliban

PROSPERO   He is as disproportion'd in his manners
             As in his shape. Go, sirrah, to my cell;
             Take with you your companions; as you look

	To have my pardon, trim it handsomely.
CALIBAN	Ay, that I will; and I'll be wise hereafter
	And seek for grace. What a thrice-double ass
	Was I, to take this drunkard for a god
	And worship this dull fool!
PROSPERO	Go to; away!
ALONSO	Hence, and bestow your luggage where you found it.
SEBASTIAN	Or stole it, rather.

Exeunt CALIBAN, STEPHANO, *and* TRINCULO

PROSPERO	Sir, I invite your highness and your train
	To my poor cell, where you shall take your rest
	For this one night; which, part of it, I'll waste
	With such discourse as, I not doubt, shall make it
	Go quick away: the story of my life
	And the particular accidents gone by
	Since I came to this isle: and in the morn
	I'll bring you to your ship and so to Naples,
	Where I have hope to see the nuptial
	Of these our dear-beloved solemnized;
	And thence retire me to my Milan, where
	Every third thought shall be my grave.
ALONSO	I long
	To hear the story of your life, which must
	Take the ear strangely.
PROSPERO	I'll deliver all;
	And promise you calm seas, auspicious gales

And sail so expeditious that shall catch
Your royal fleet far off.

[*Aside to* ARIEL]

My Ariel, chick,
That is thy charge: then to the elements
Be free, and fare thou well! Please you, draw near.

Exeunt

PROSPERO   Now my charms are all o'erthrown,
And what strength I have's mine own,
Which is most faint: now, 'tis true,
I must be here confined by you,
Or sent to Naples. Let me not,
Since I have my dukedom got
And pardon'd the deceiver, dwell
In this bare island by your spell;
But release me from my bands
With the help of your good hands:
Gentle breath of yours my sails
Must fill, or else my project fails,
Which was to please. Now I want
Spirits to enforce, art to enchant,
And my ending is despair,
Unless I be relieved by prayer,
Which pierces so that it assaults
Mercy itself and frees all faults.
As you from crimes would pardon'd be,
Let your indulgence set me free.

WILLIAM SHAKESPEARE was born in 1564 in Stratford-upon-Avon to John Shakespeare, an alderman and glove-maker, and Mary Arden, the daughter of a land-owner. He married Anne Hathaway at the age of eighteen, and six months later Anne gave birth to a daughter Susannah and later to twins Hamnet and Judith, though Hamnet died at the age of just 11. Shakespeare had a successful career in London and was a hugely prolific writer with 39 plays and 154 sonnets attributed to him. He retired at the age of 49, moving back to Stratford-upon-Avon, and died aged 52.

RECOMMENDED PLAYS BY WILLIAM SHAKESPEARE:

Hamlet
Antony and Cleopatra
Othello

VINTAGE MINIS

The Vintage Minis bring you the world's greatest writers on the experiences that make us human. These stylish, entertaining little books explore the whole spectrum of life – from birth to death, and everything in between. Which means there's something here for everyone, whatever your story.

vintageminis.co.uk